BIG SISTER COCO

THE BIRTHDAY SURPRISE

Story by
Jesse Byrd

Illustrations by
Lau Moraiti

To my little brother, Isaiah
—Jesse

To my loves, who inspire
me to chase my dreams
—Lau

Text Copyright © 2023 Jesse Byrd
Illustration Copyright © 2023 Laura Moraiti

Book and Cover Design by Lau Moraiti
9781223187075 Hardcover English
9781223187082 Paperback English

Published by Paw Prints Publishing
PawPrintsPublishing.com
Printed in China

1.

Where Is
Bo's Present?

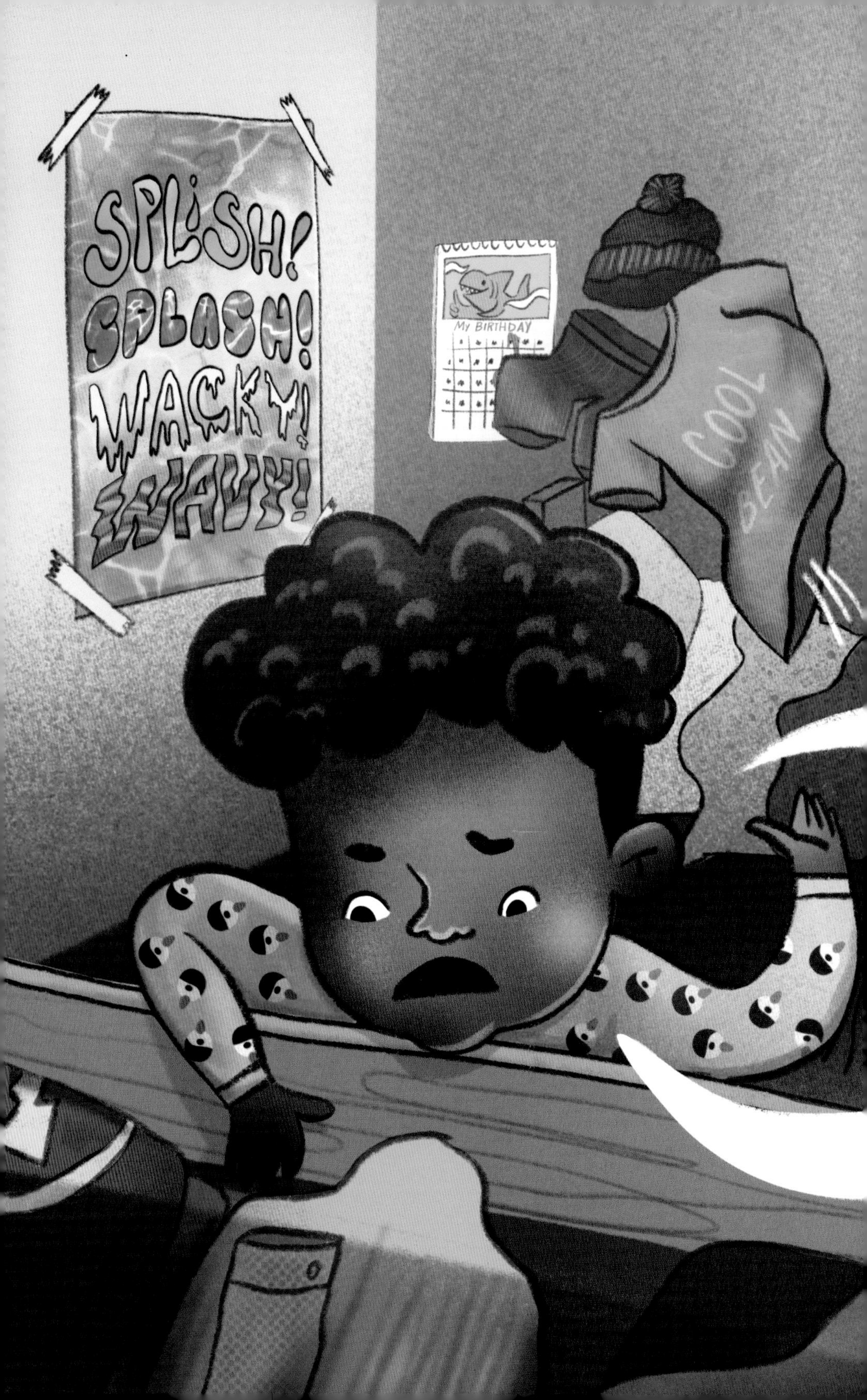
SPLISH!
SPLASH!
WACKY!
WAVY!
MY BIRTHDAY
COOL BEAN

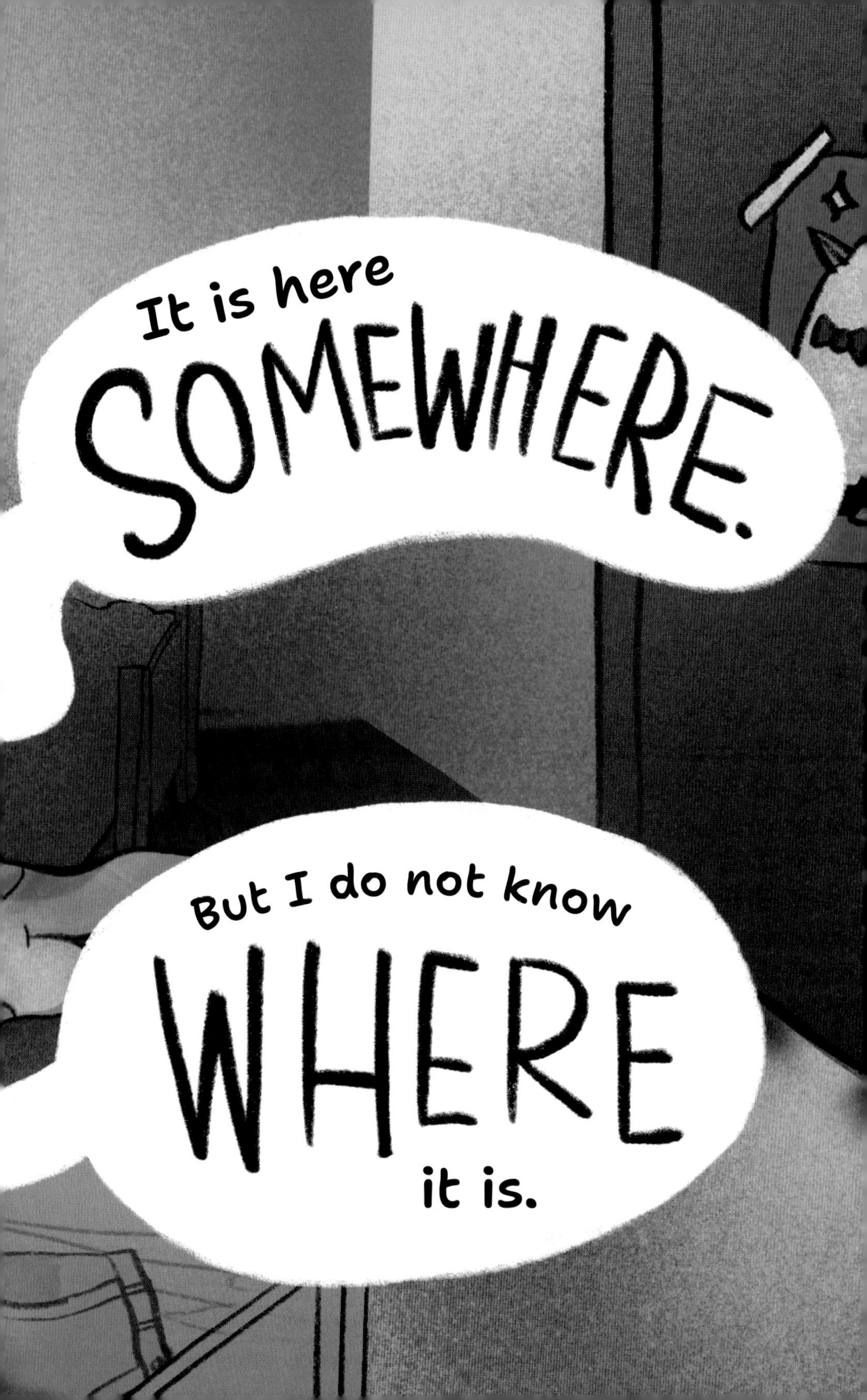
It is here SOMEWHERE.
But I do not know WHERE it is.

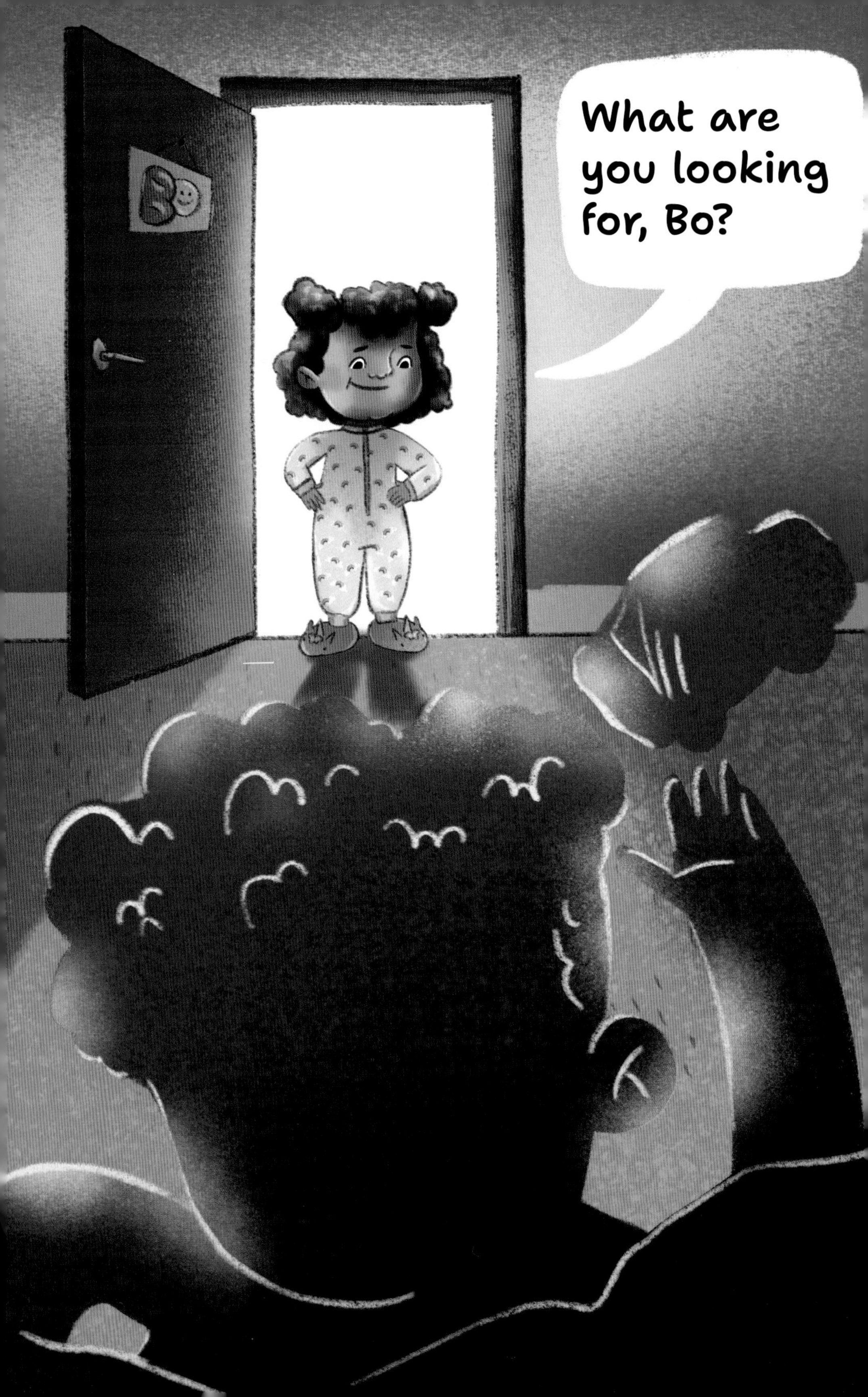
What are you looking for, Bo?

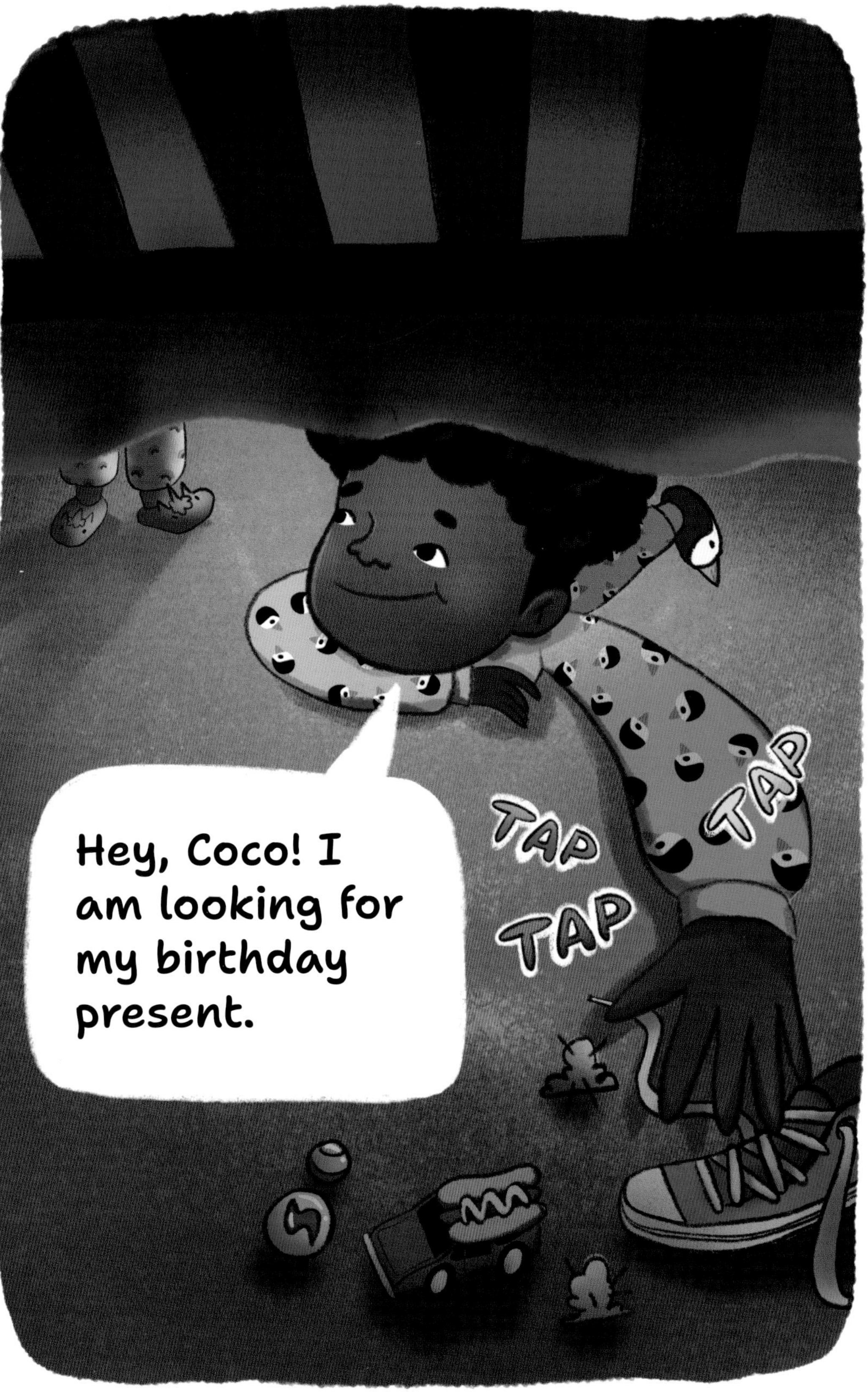
Hey, Coco! I am looking for my birthday present.
TAP
TAP
TAP

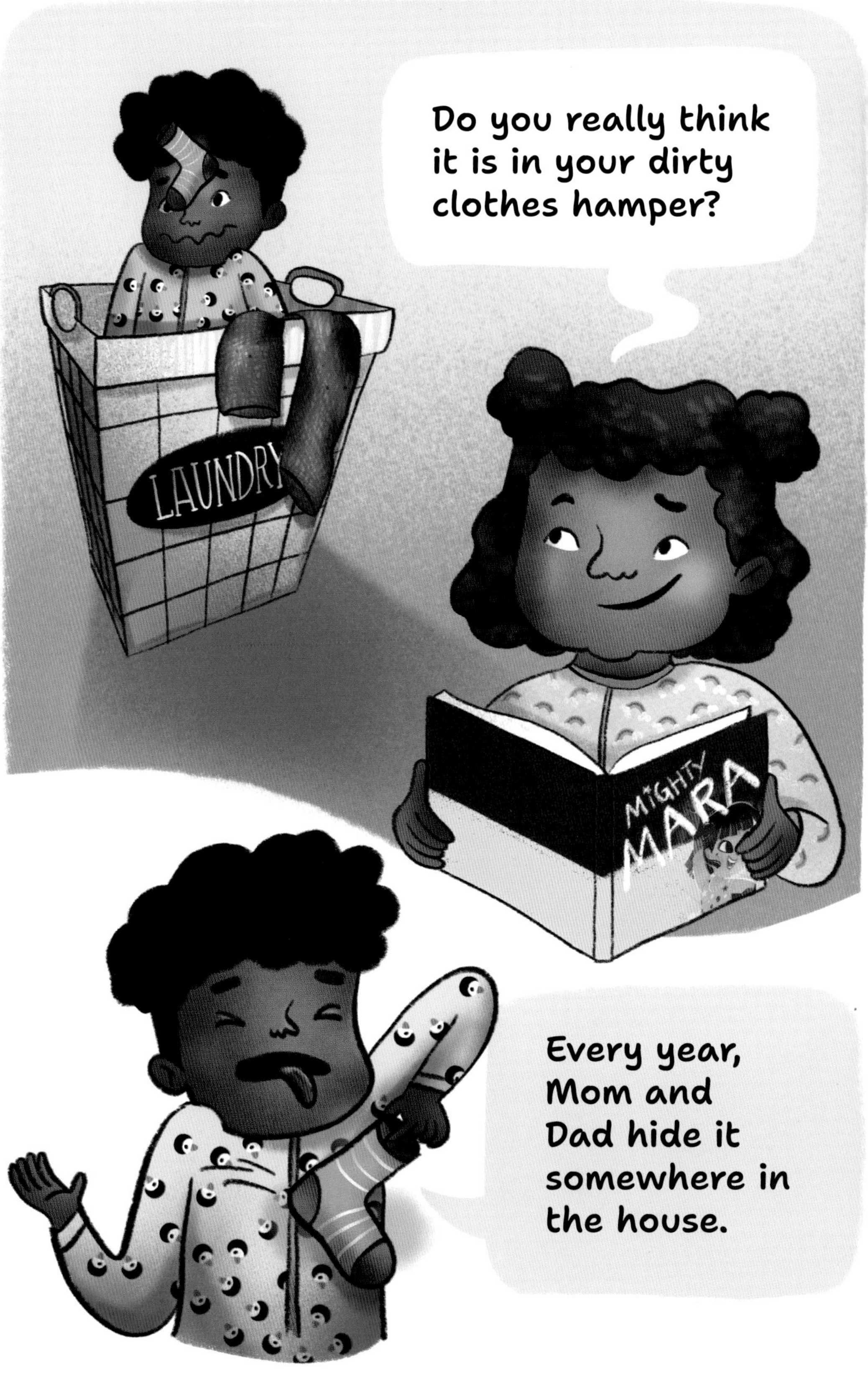
LAUNDRY
Do you really think it is in your dirty clothes hamper?
MIGHTY MARA
Every year, Mom and Dad hide it somewhere in the house.

Coco, you are good at finding things. Will you help me find my present?

Of course, Bo! This will be fun.

My first question is...

Where are Mom and Dad's favorite places to hide when we play hide-and-seek?

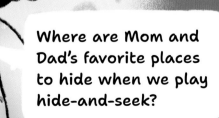

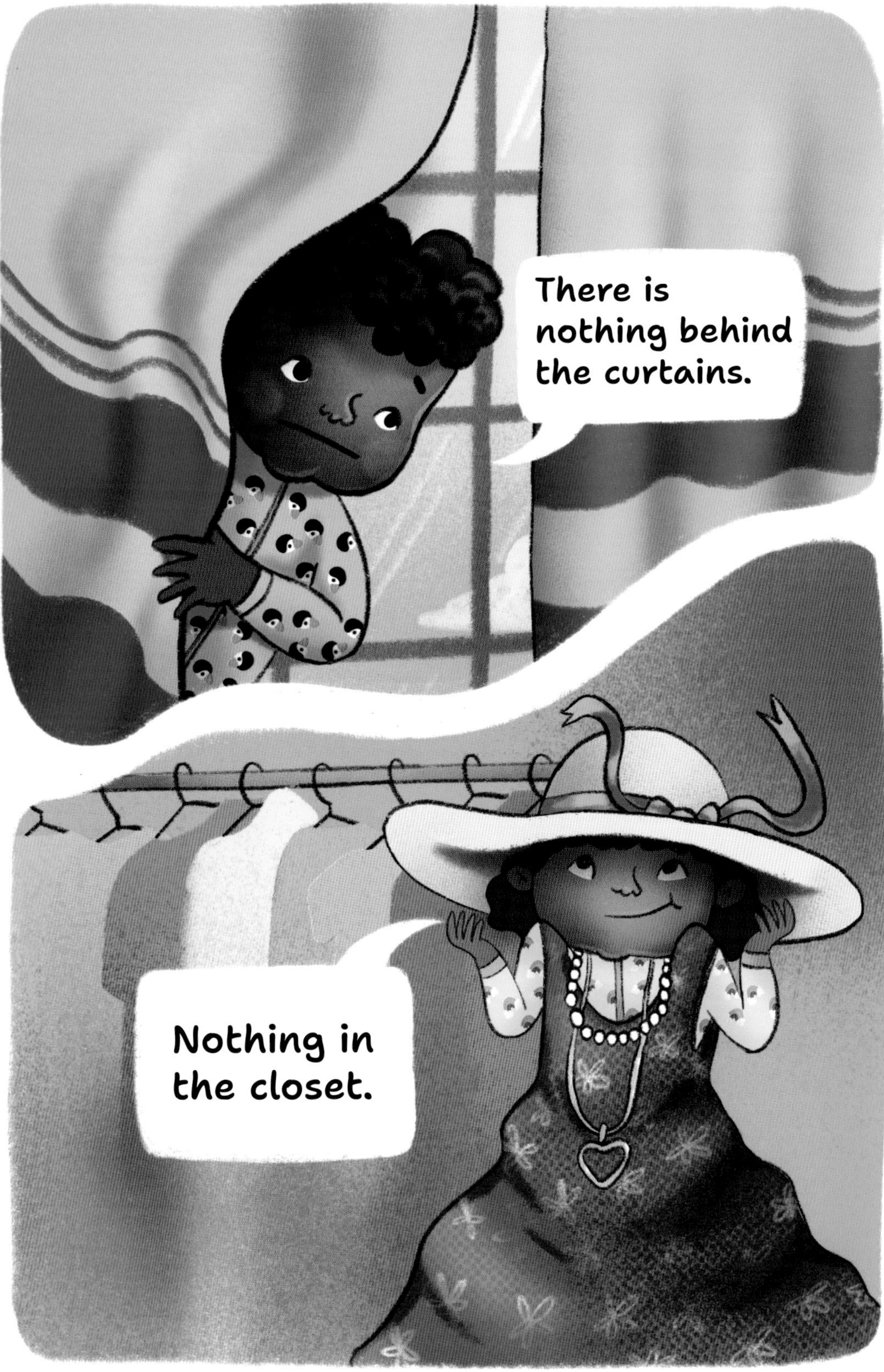
There is nothing behind the curtains.
Nothing in the closet.

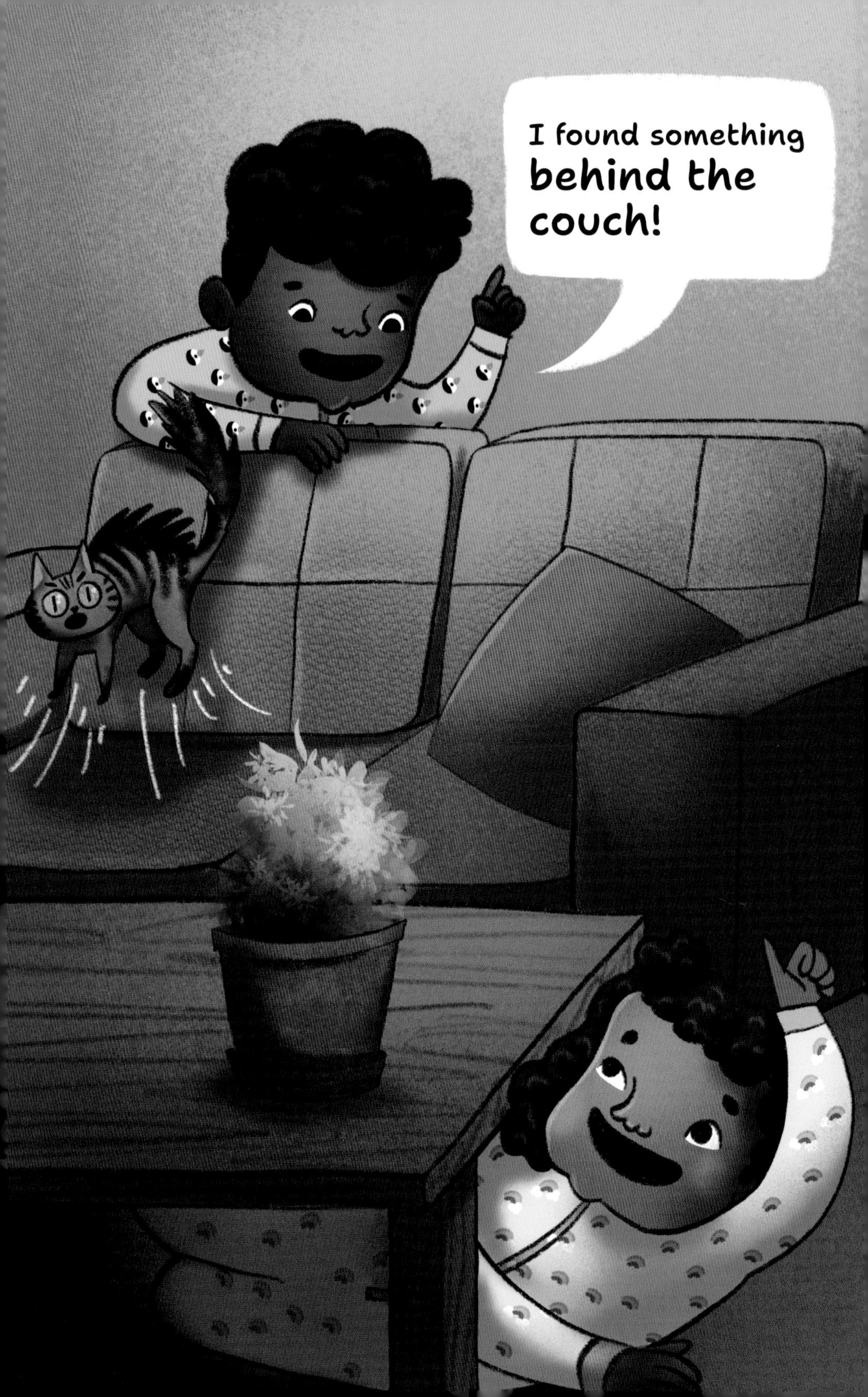
I found something behind the couch!

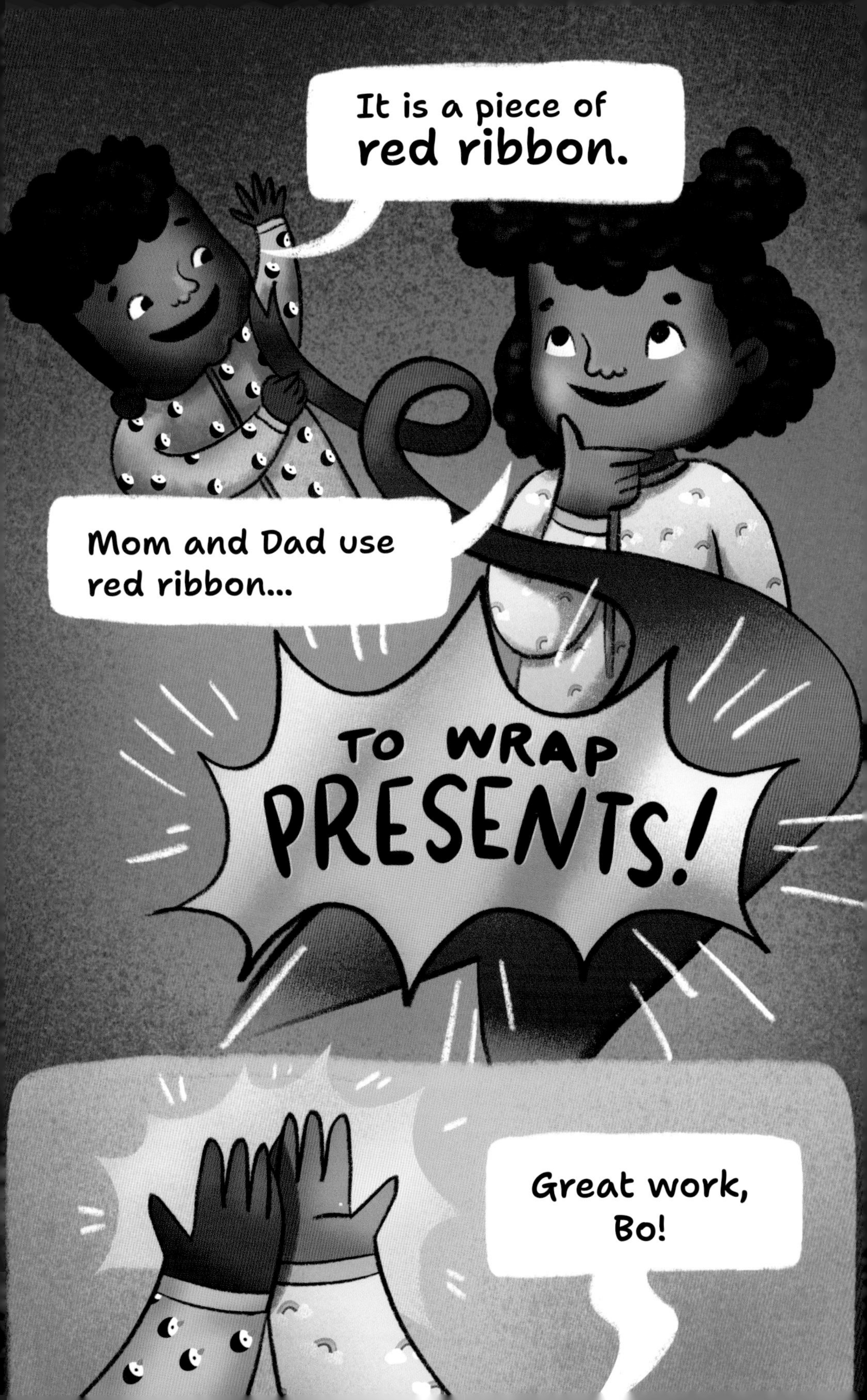
It is a piece of
red ribbon.
Mom and Dad use
red ribbon...
TO WRAP
PRESENTS!
Great work,
Bo!

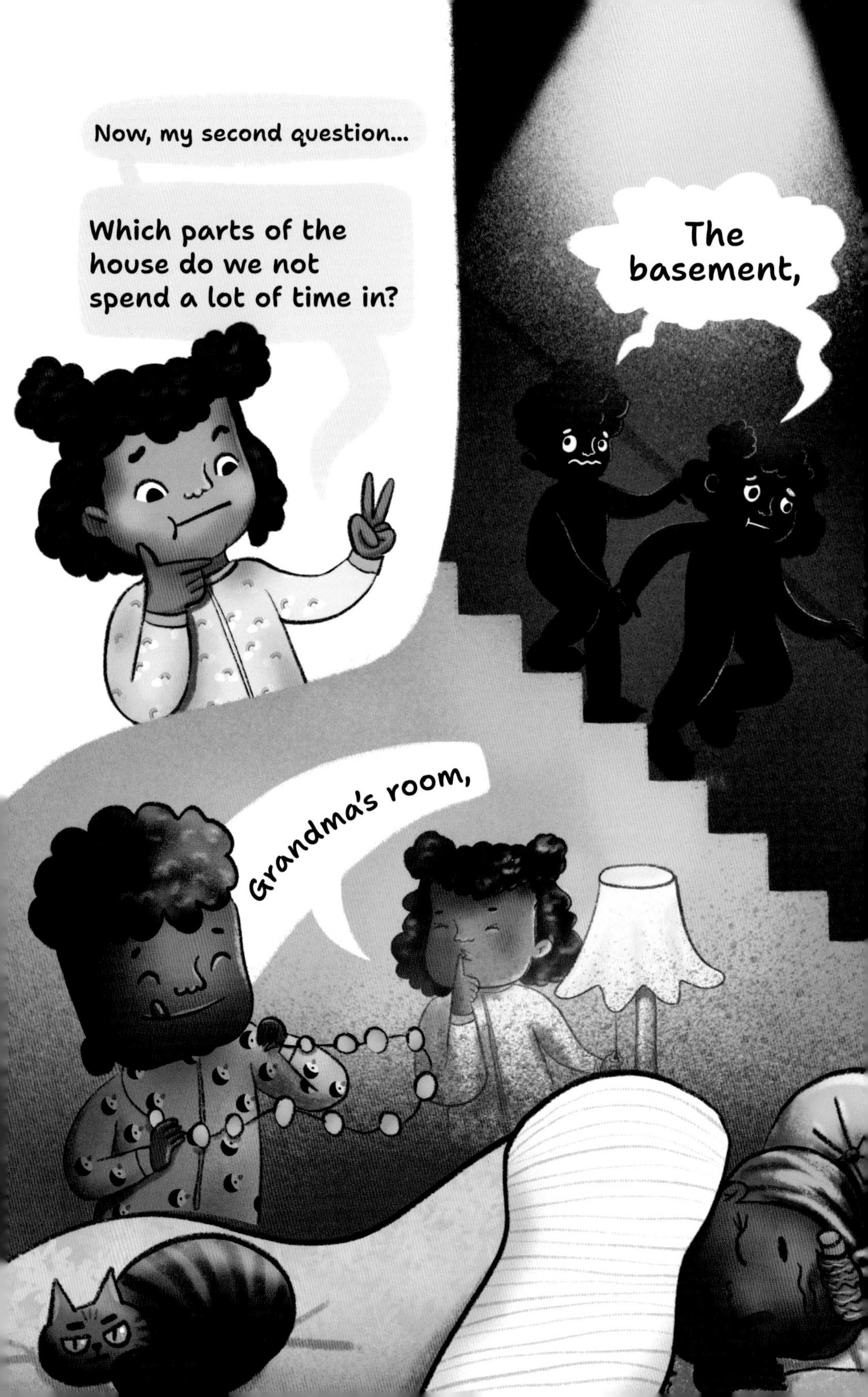
Now, my second question...
Which parts of the house do we not spend a lot of time in?
The basement,
Grandma's room,

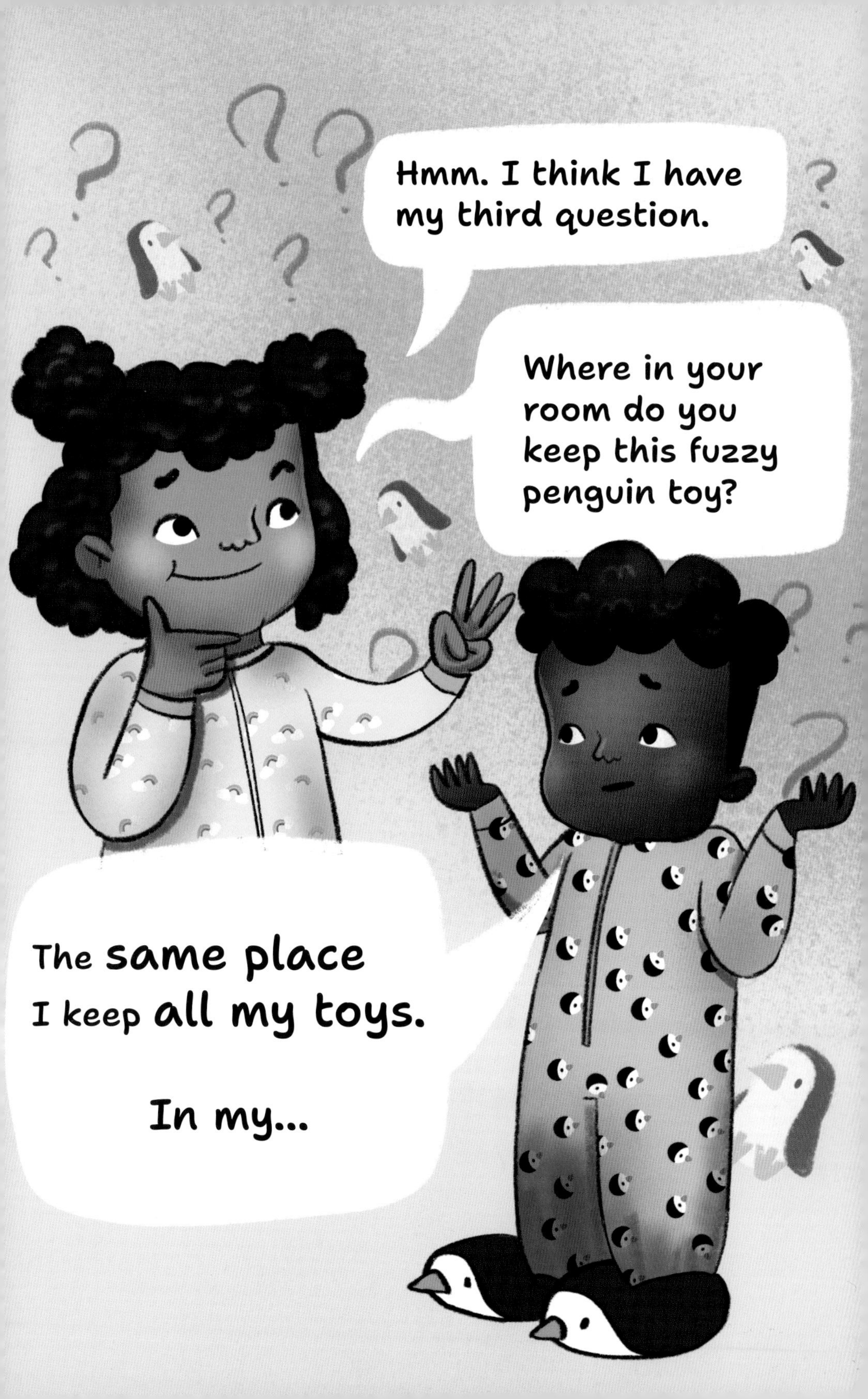
Hmm. I think I have my third question.
Where in your room do you keep this fuzzy penguin toy?
The same place I keep all my toys.
In my...

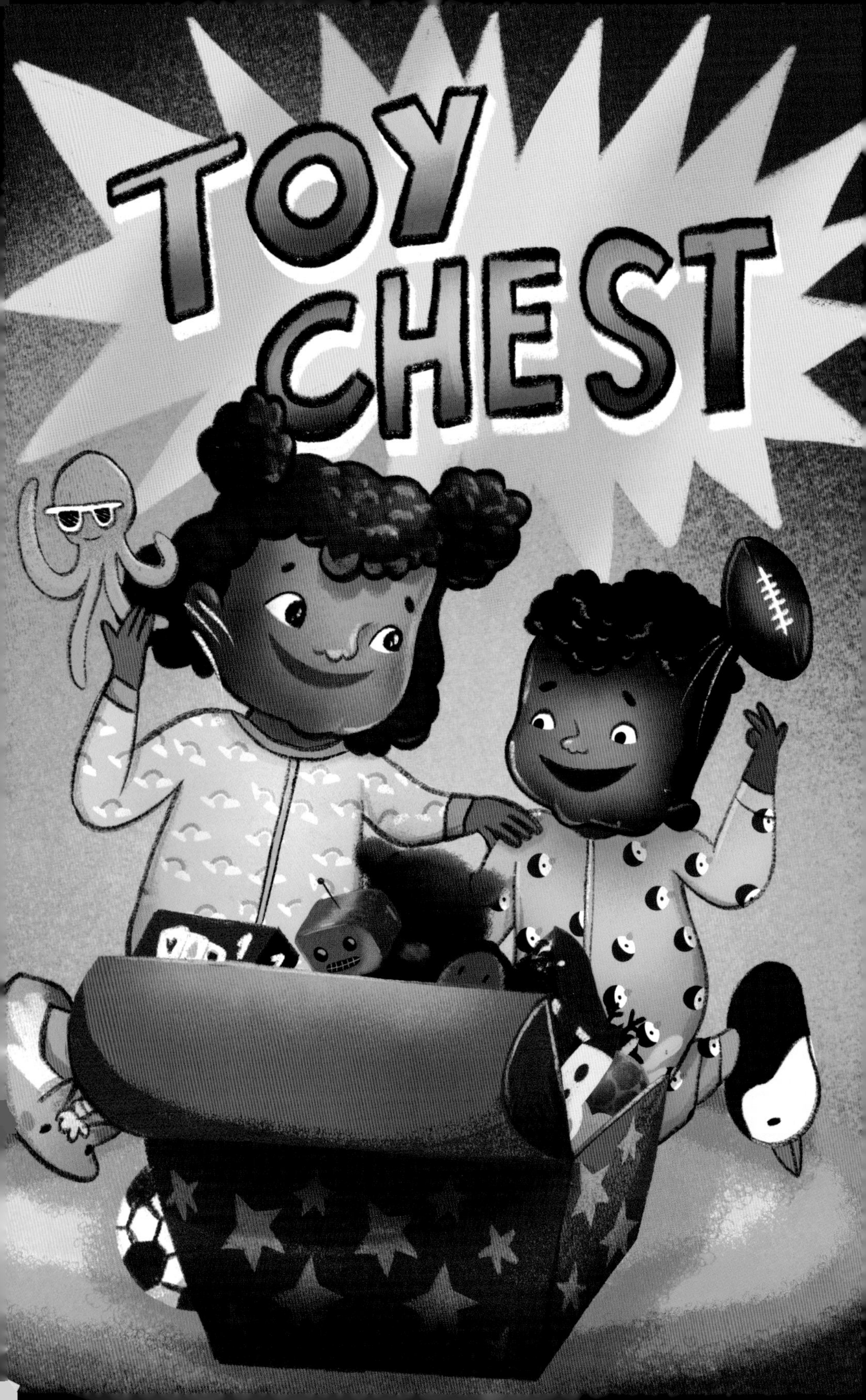
TOY
CHEST

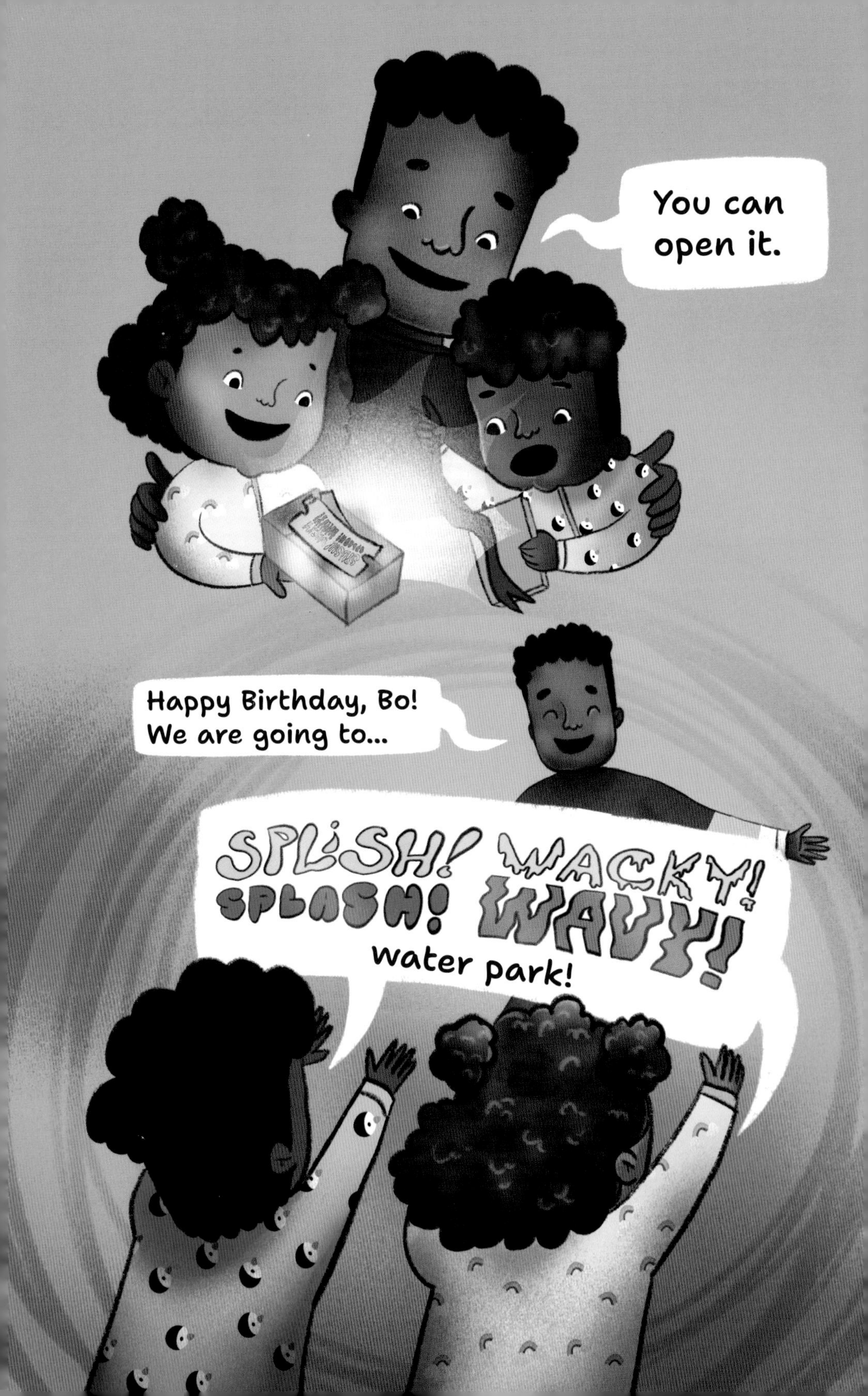
You can open it.
Happy Birthday, Bo! We are going to...
SPLISH! SPLASH! WACKY! WAVY! water park!

2.

What Should We Bring?

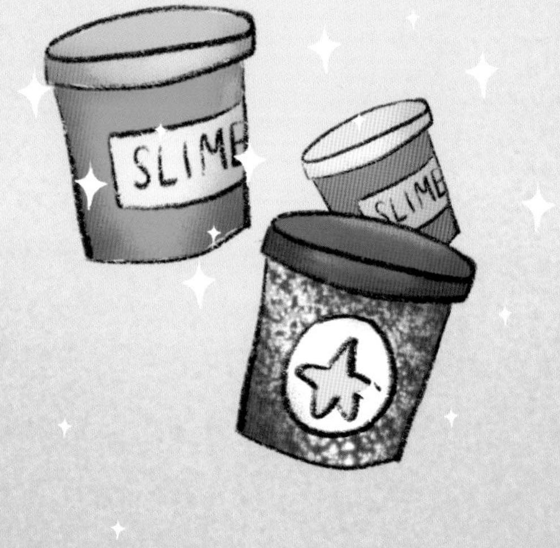
SLIME
SLIME

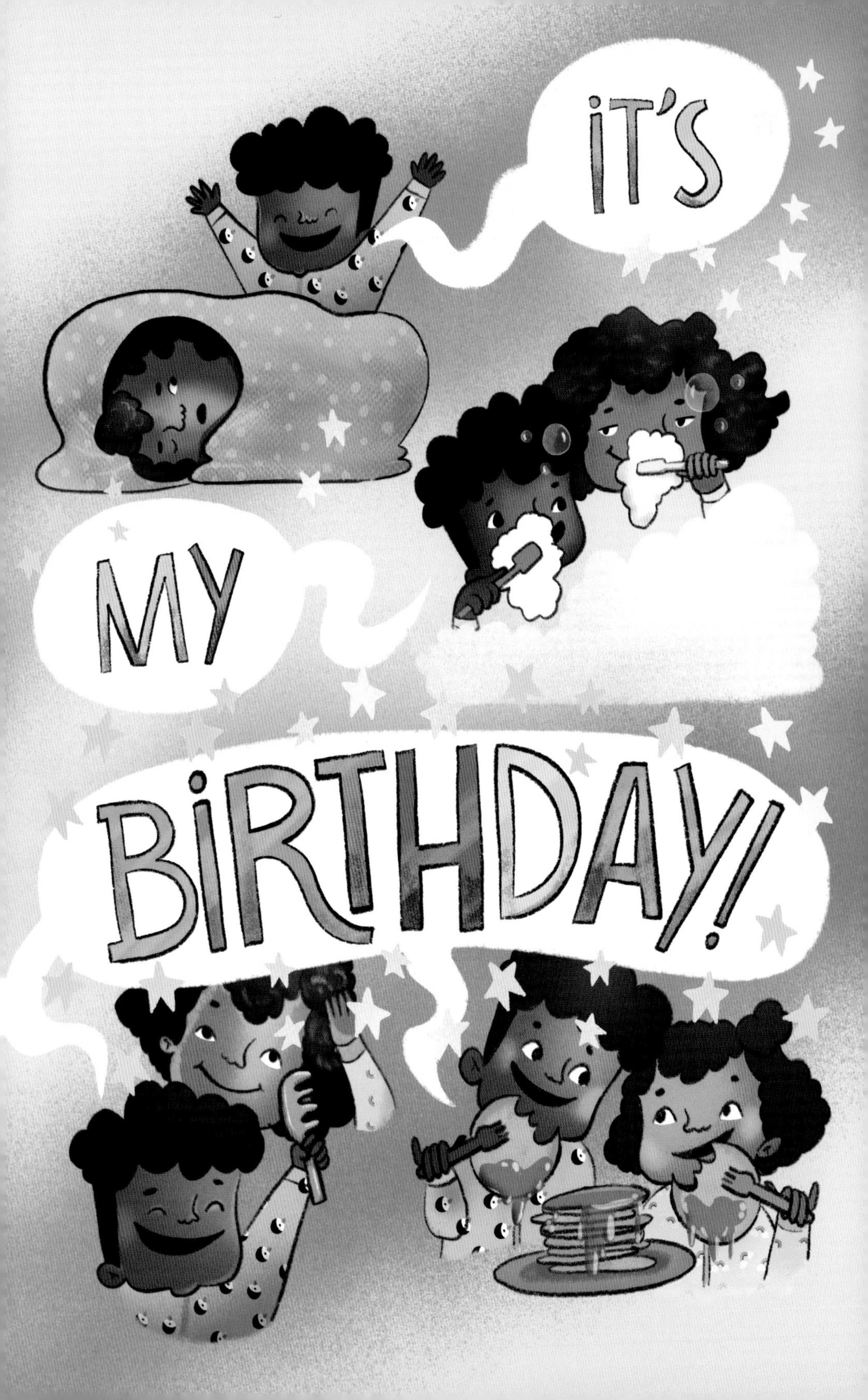
IT'S
MY
BIRTHDAY!

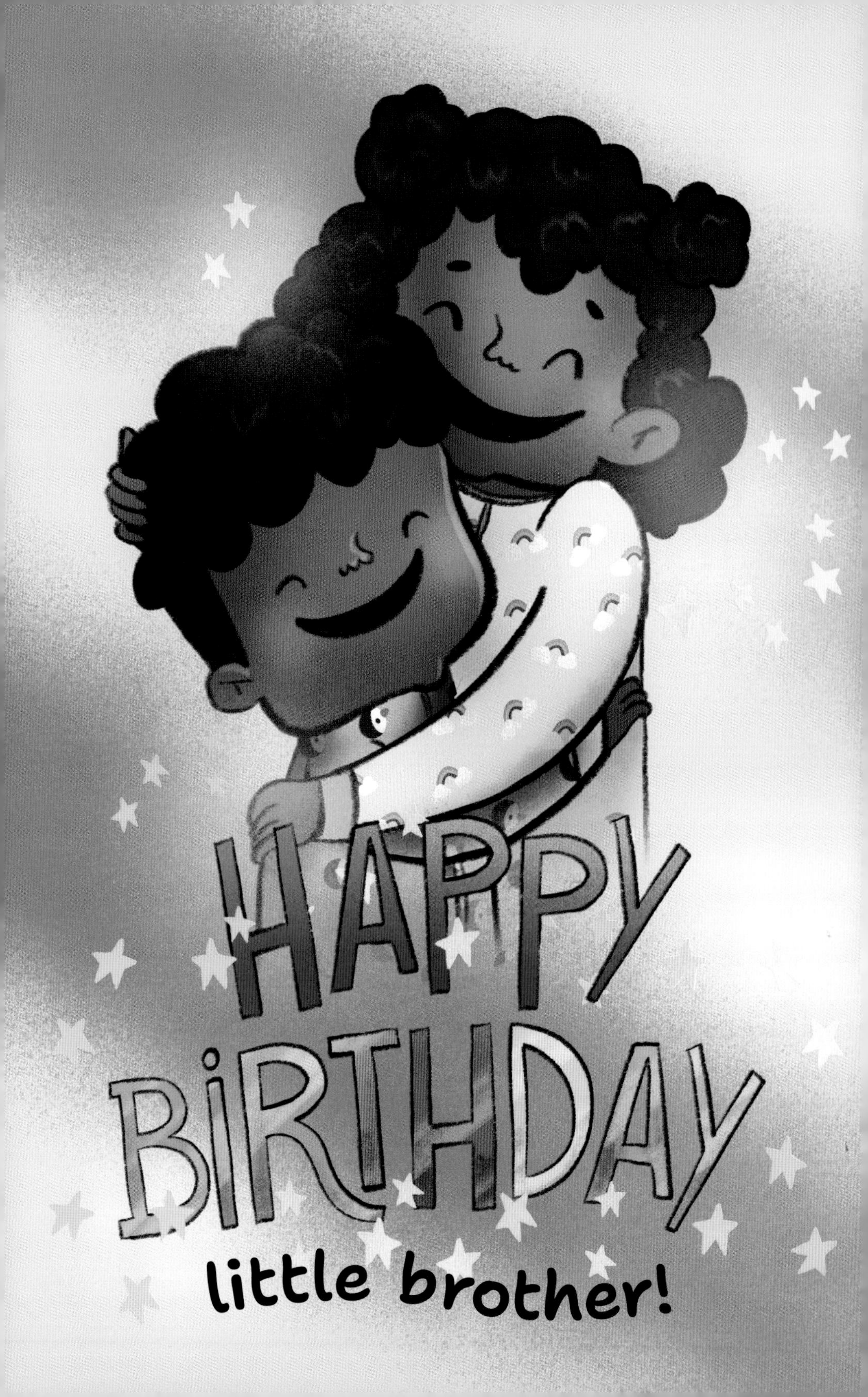
HAPPY BiRTHDAY
little brother!

We are going to
SPLISH! SPLASH!
But wait. What do people bring to a water park?

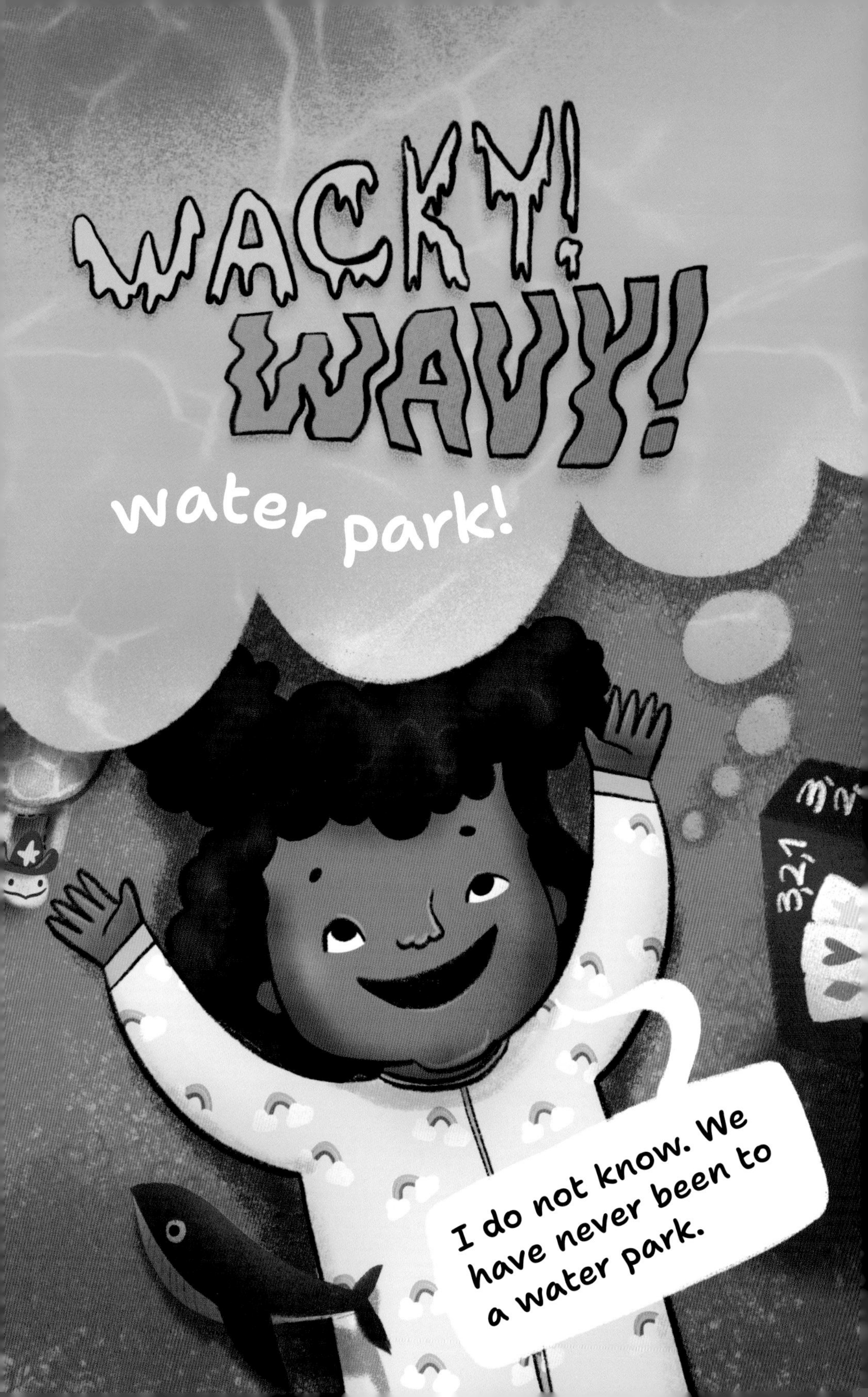
WACKY! WAVY!
water park!
3,2,1
I do not know. We have never been to a water park.

What did you pack?
NOTHING
I wanted to see what you packed first.
We can figure this out together.

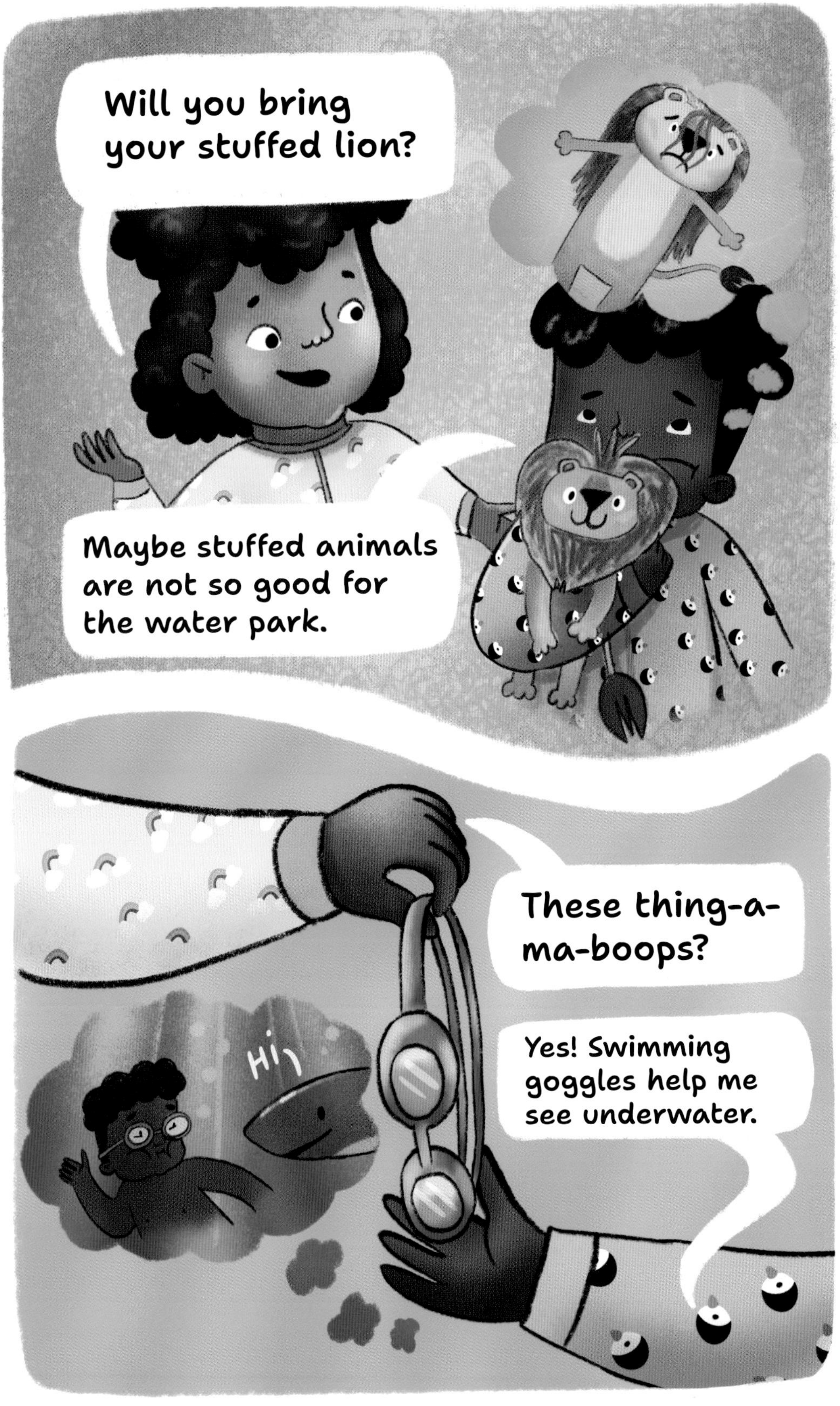
Will you bring your stuffed lion?
Maybe stuffed animals are not so good for the water park.
These thing-a-ma-boops?
Yes! Swimming goggles help me see underwater.
Hi

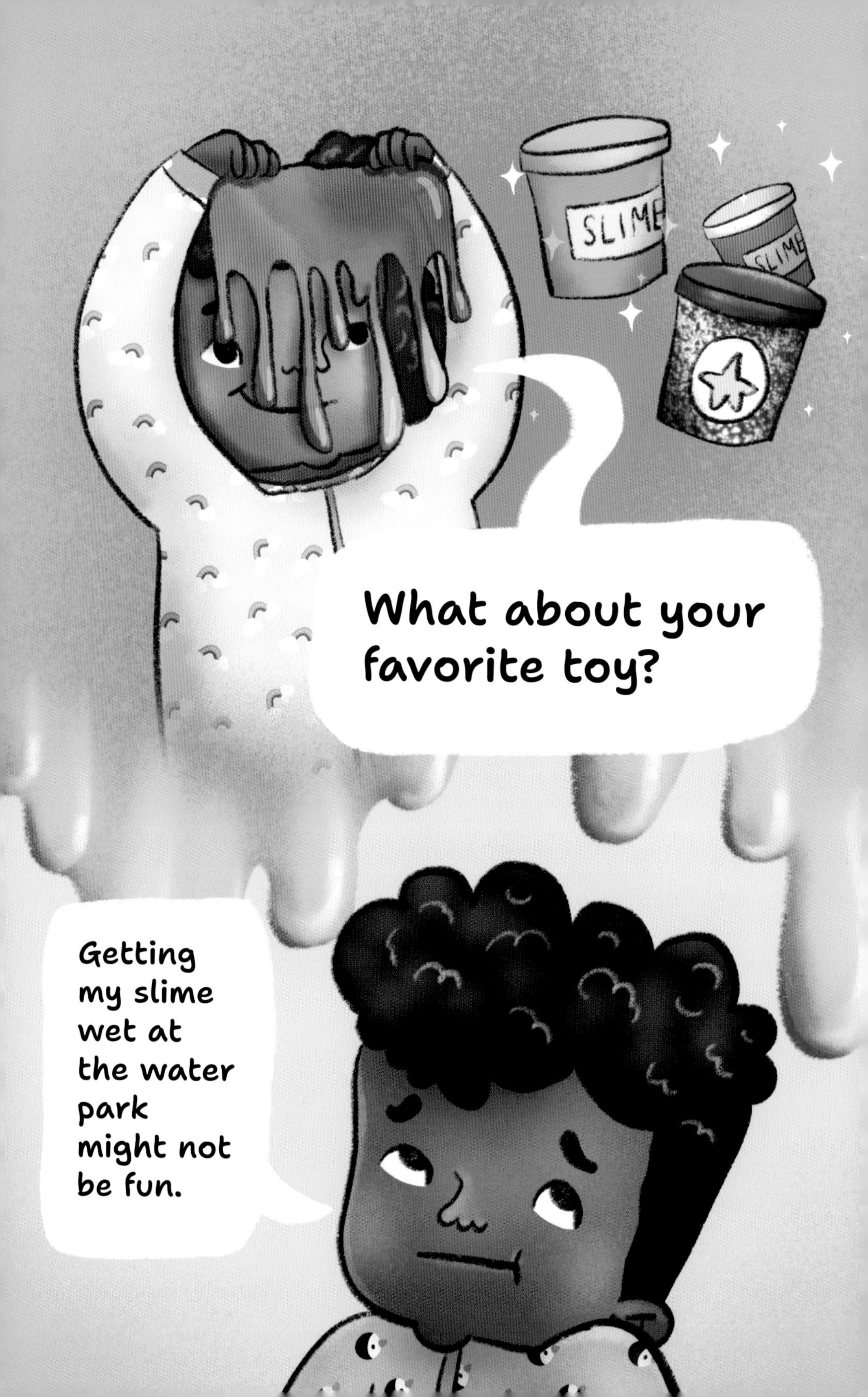
SLIME
SLIME
What about your favorite toy?
Getting my slime wet at the water park might not be fun.

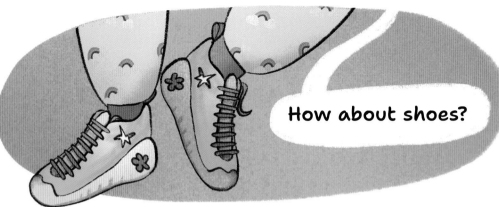

How about shoes?

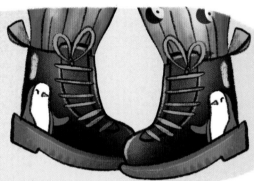

Yes! But maybe shoes that I can get wet.

How about these?

These are PERFECT!

Wait, how did you know these were in my closet?

I borrow your stuff **a lot.**

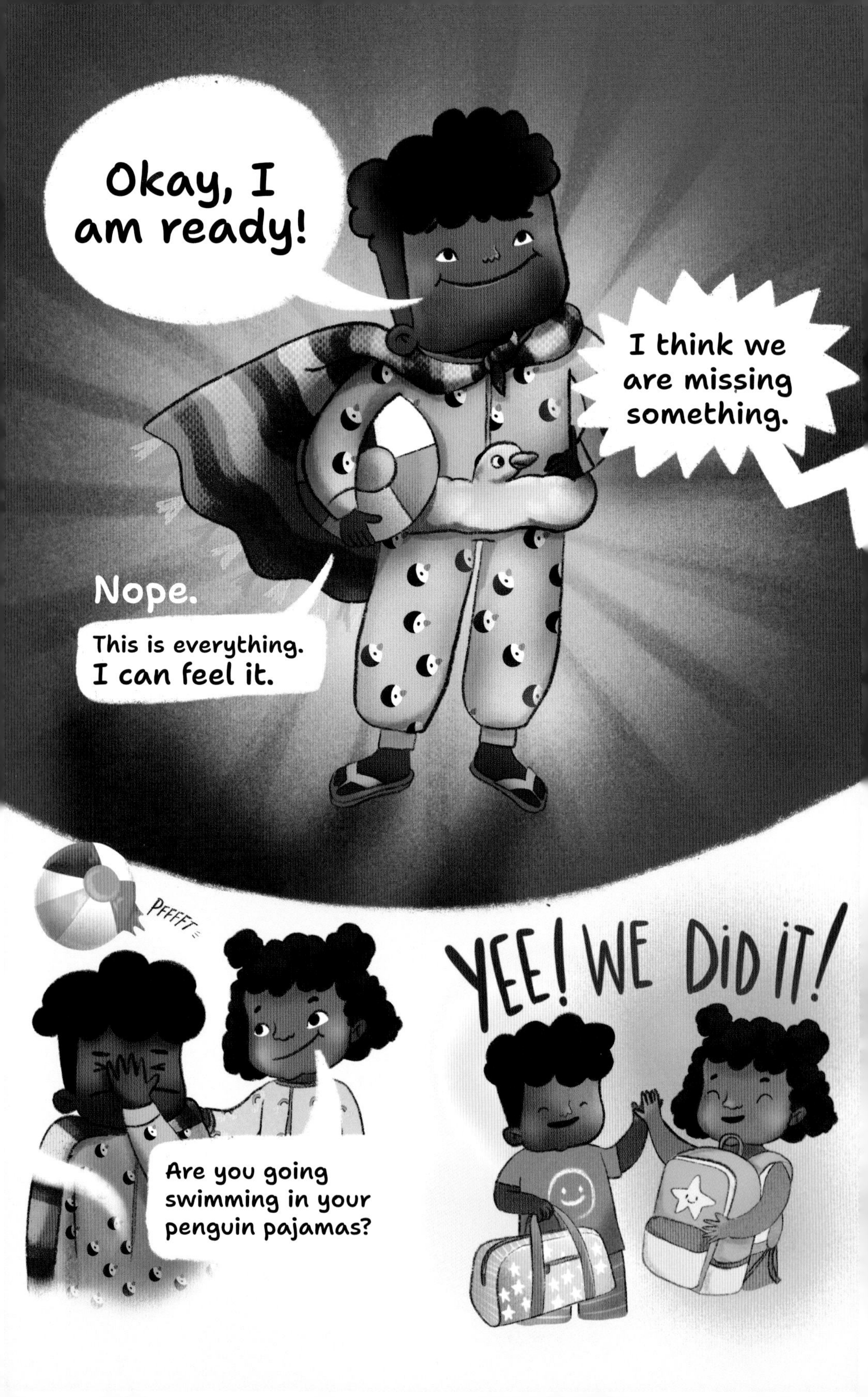
Okay, I am ready!
I think we are missing something.
Nope.
This is everything. I can feel it.
PFFFFT
Are you going swimming in your penguin pajamas?
YEE! WE DID IT!

3.

Which Slide Should We Ride?

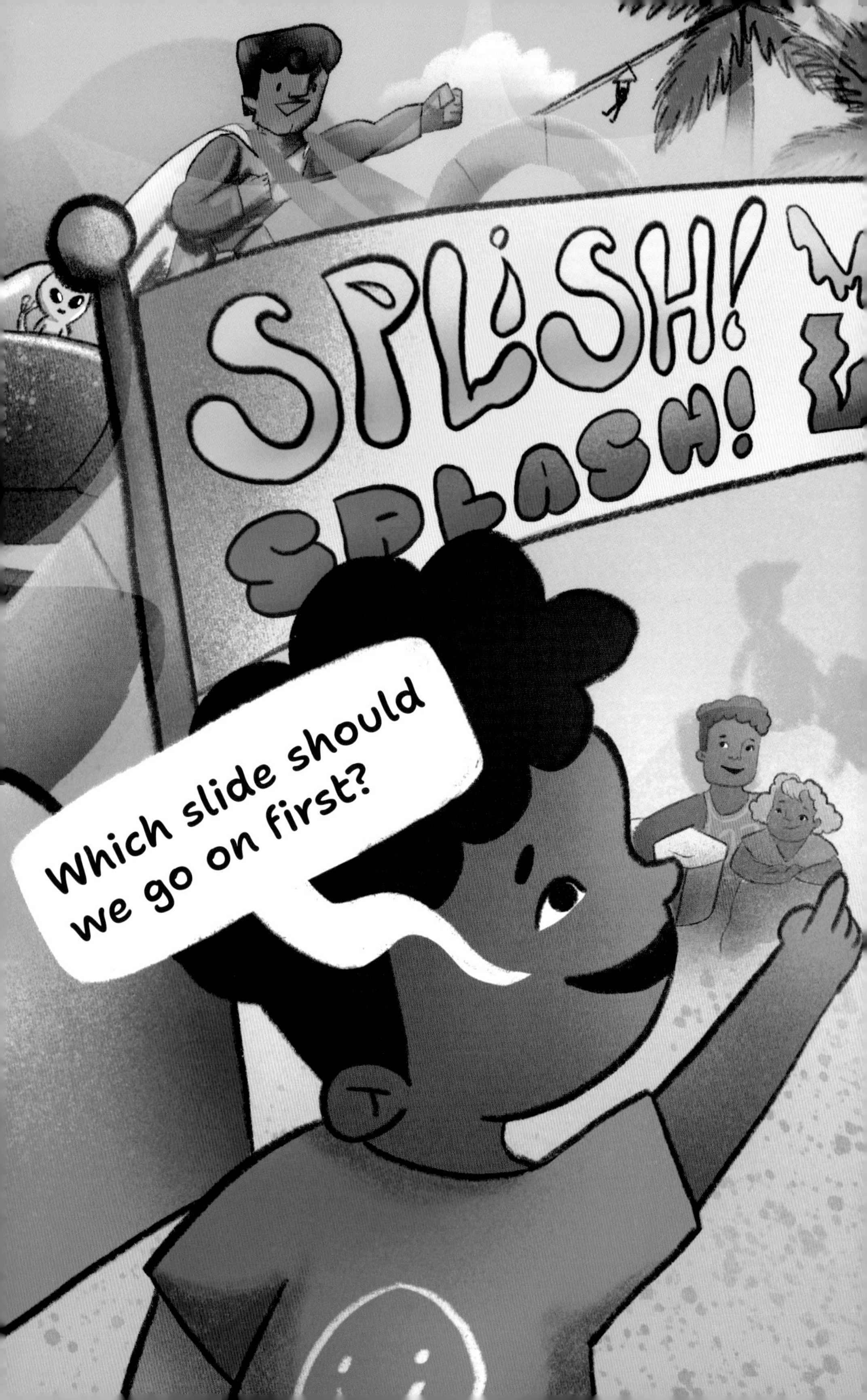
SPLISH! SPLASH!
Which slide should we go on first?

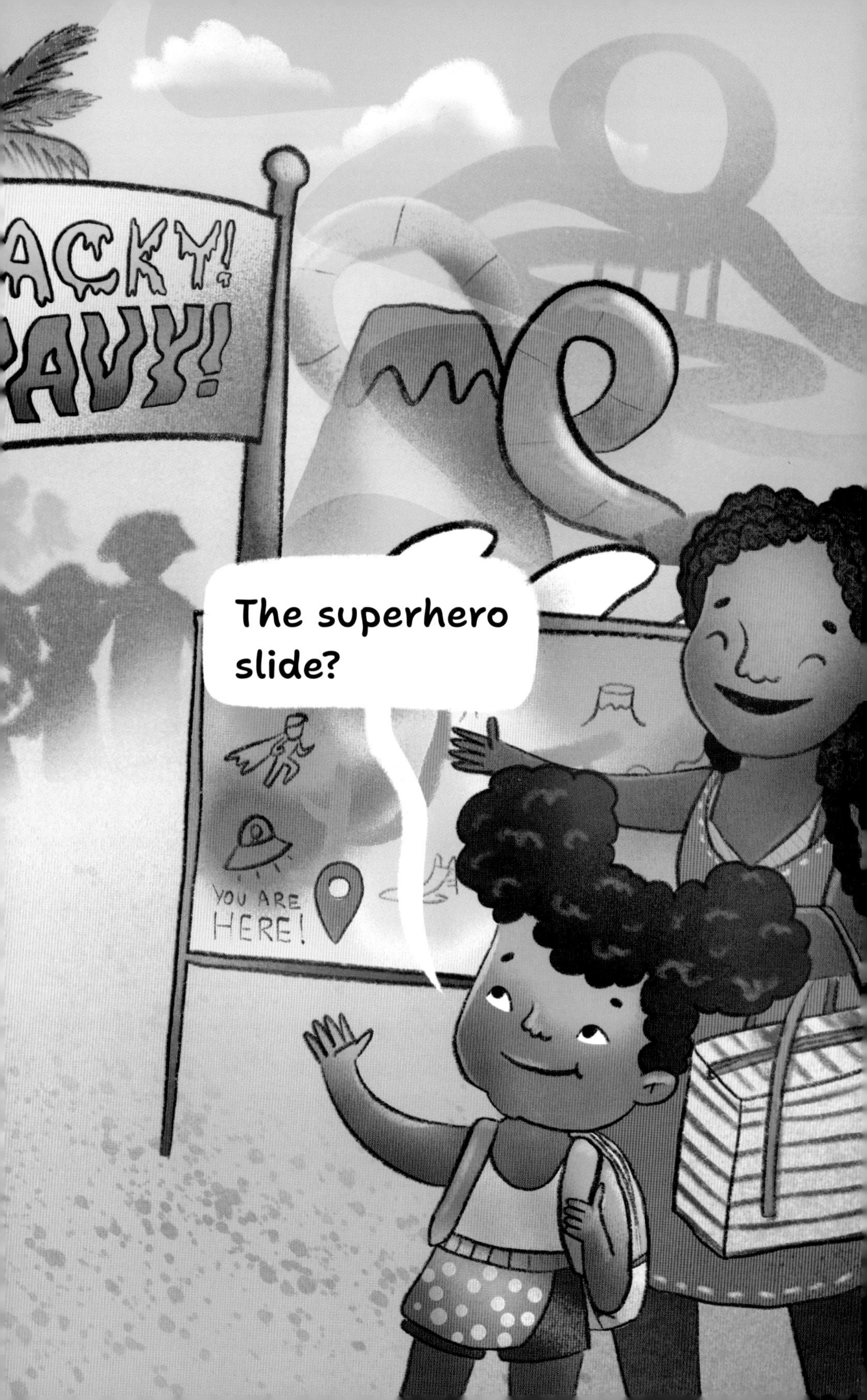
The superhero slide?
YOU ARE HERE!

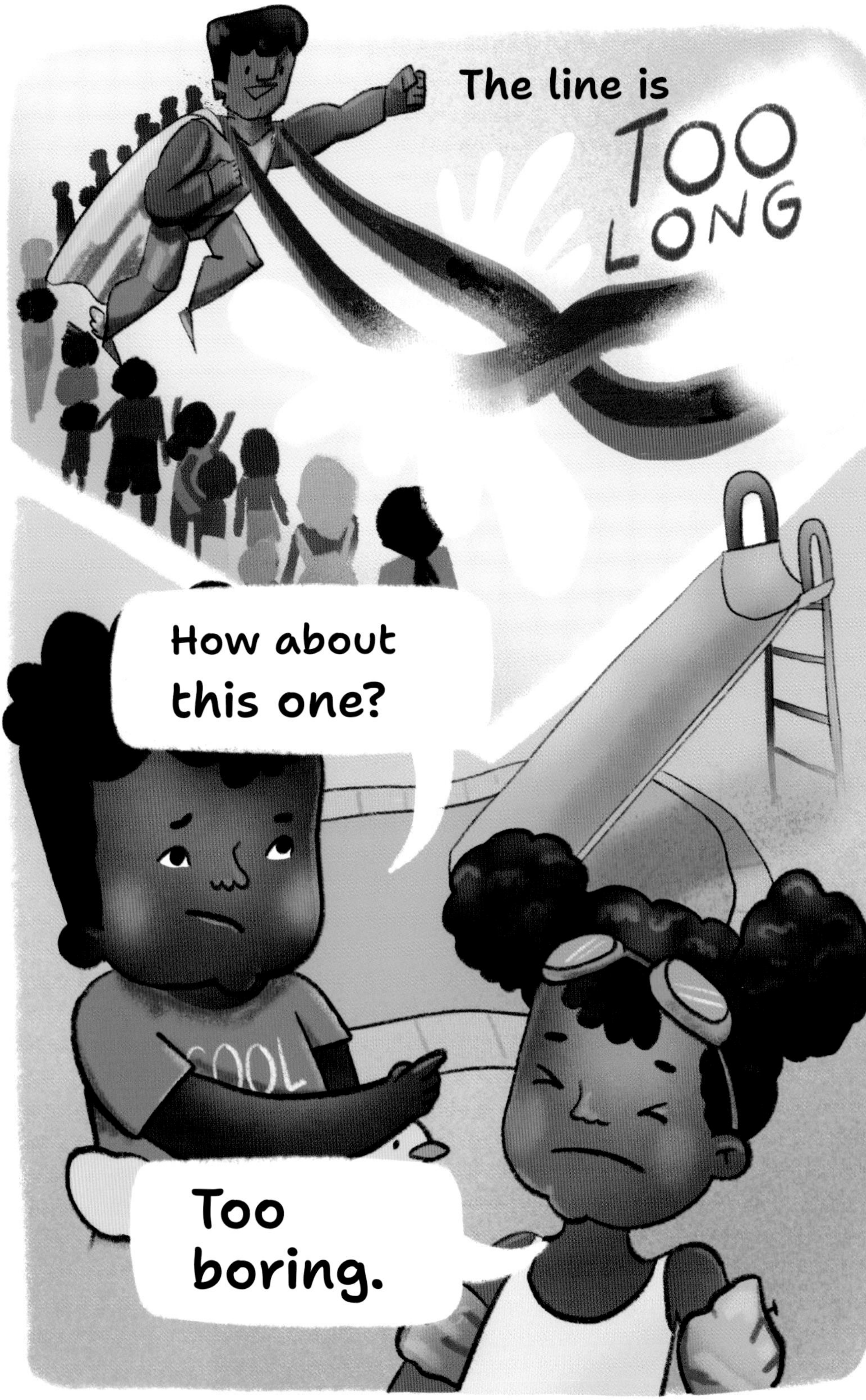
The line is TOO LONG
How about this one?
COOL
Too boring.

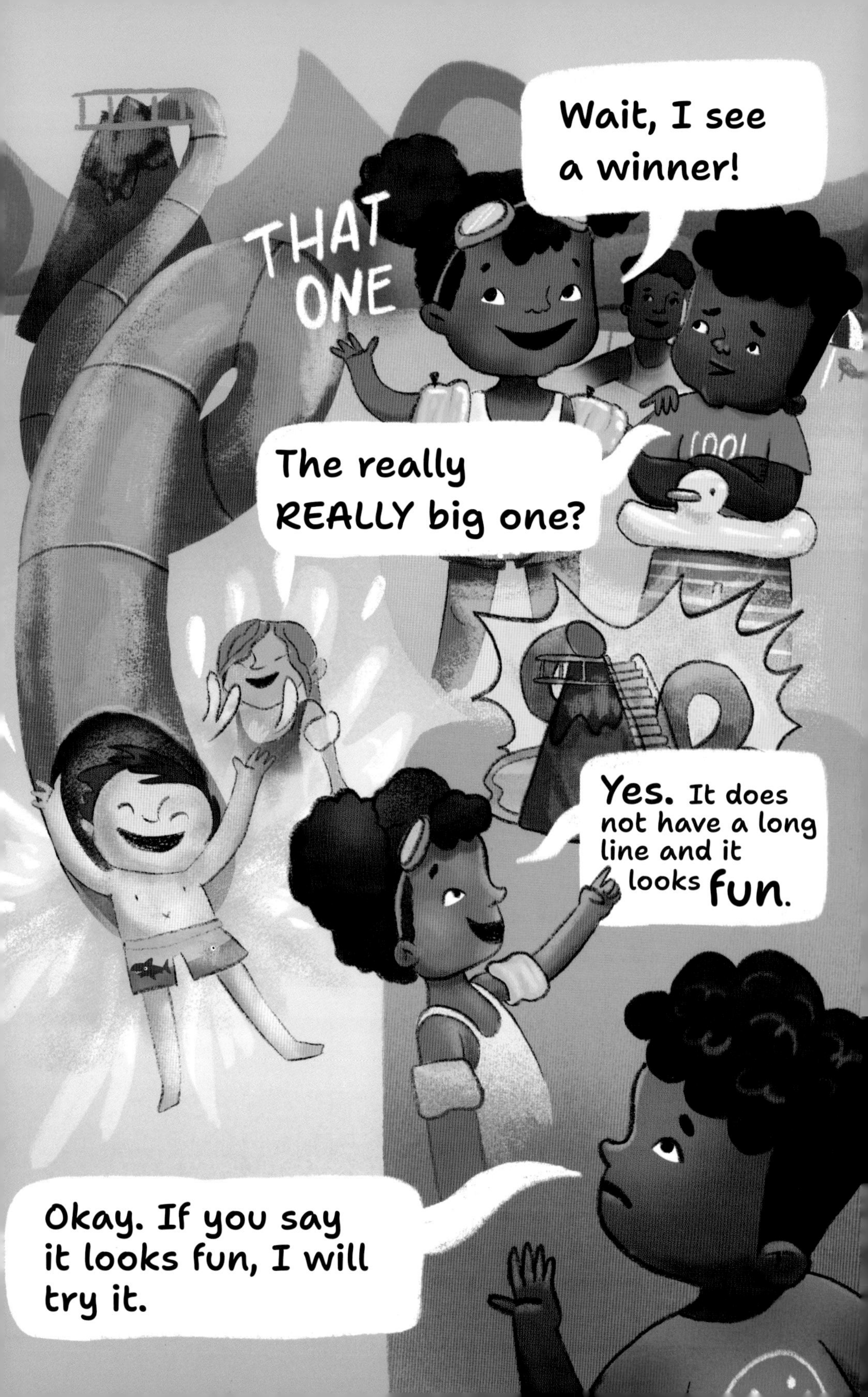
Wait, I see a winner!
THAT ONE
The really REALLY big one?
Yes. It does not have a long line and it looks fun.
Okay. If you say it looks fun, I will try it.

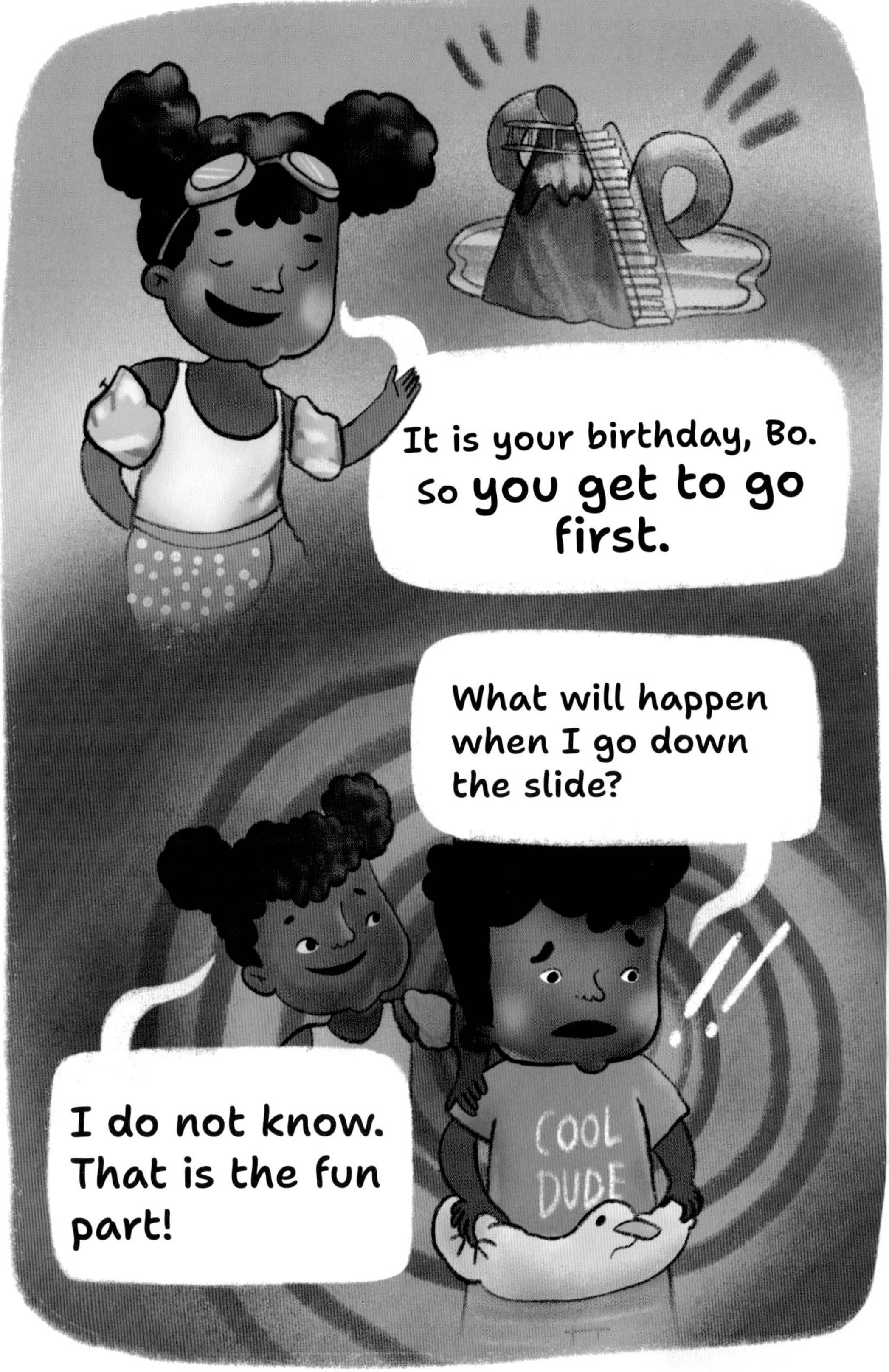
It is your birthday, Bo. So you get to go first.
What will happen when I go down the slide?
I do not know. That is the fun part!
COOL DUDE

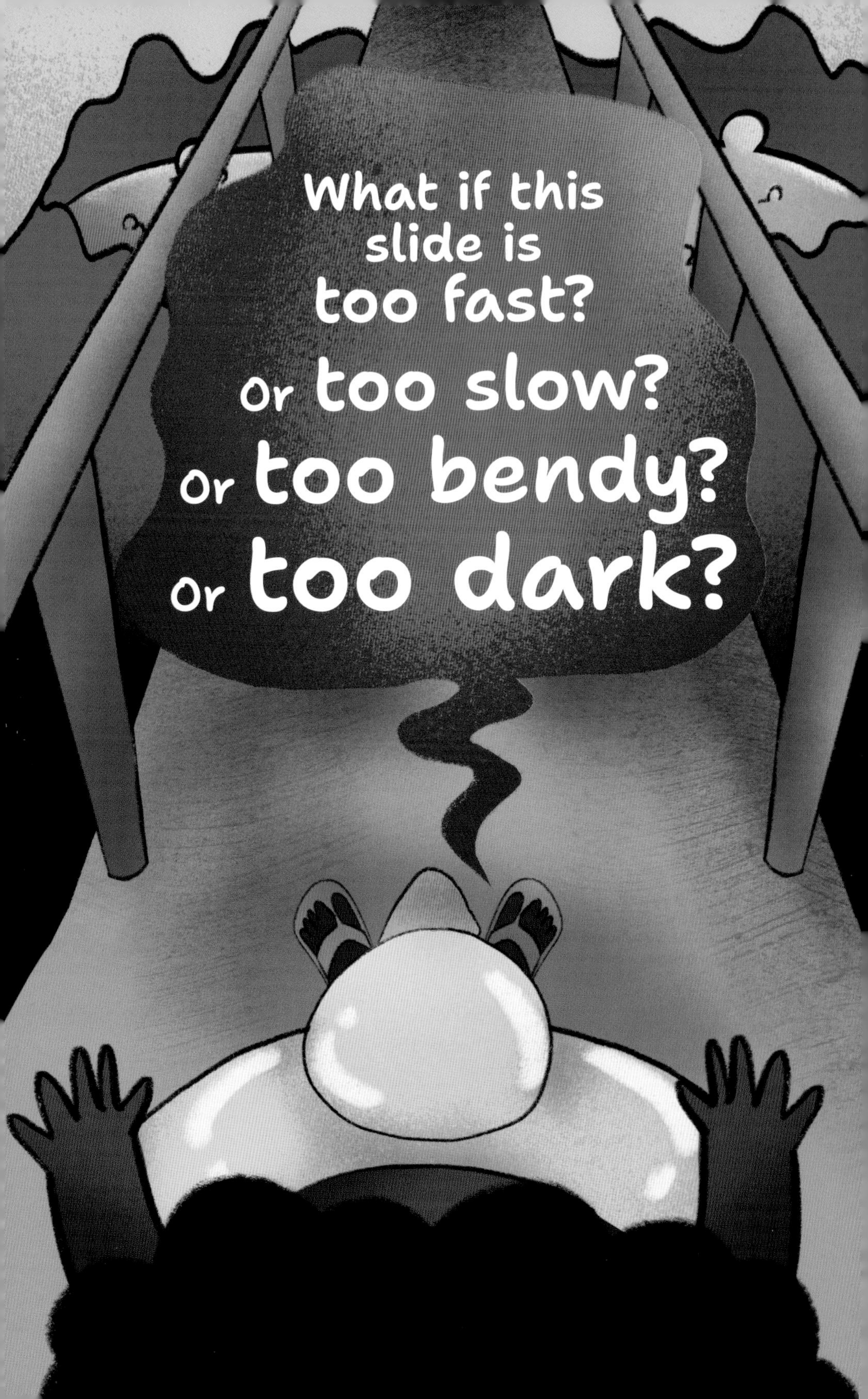
What if this
slide is
too fast?
Or too slow?
Or too bendy?
Or too dark?

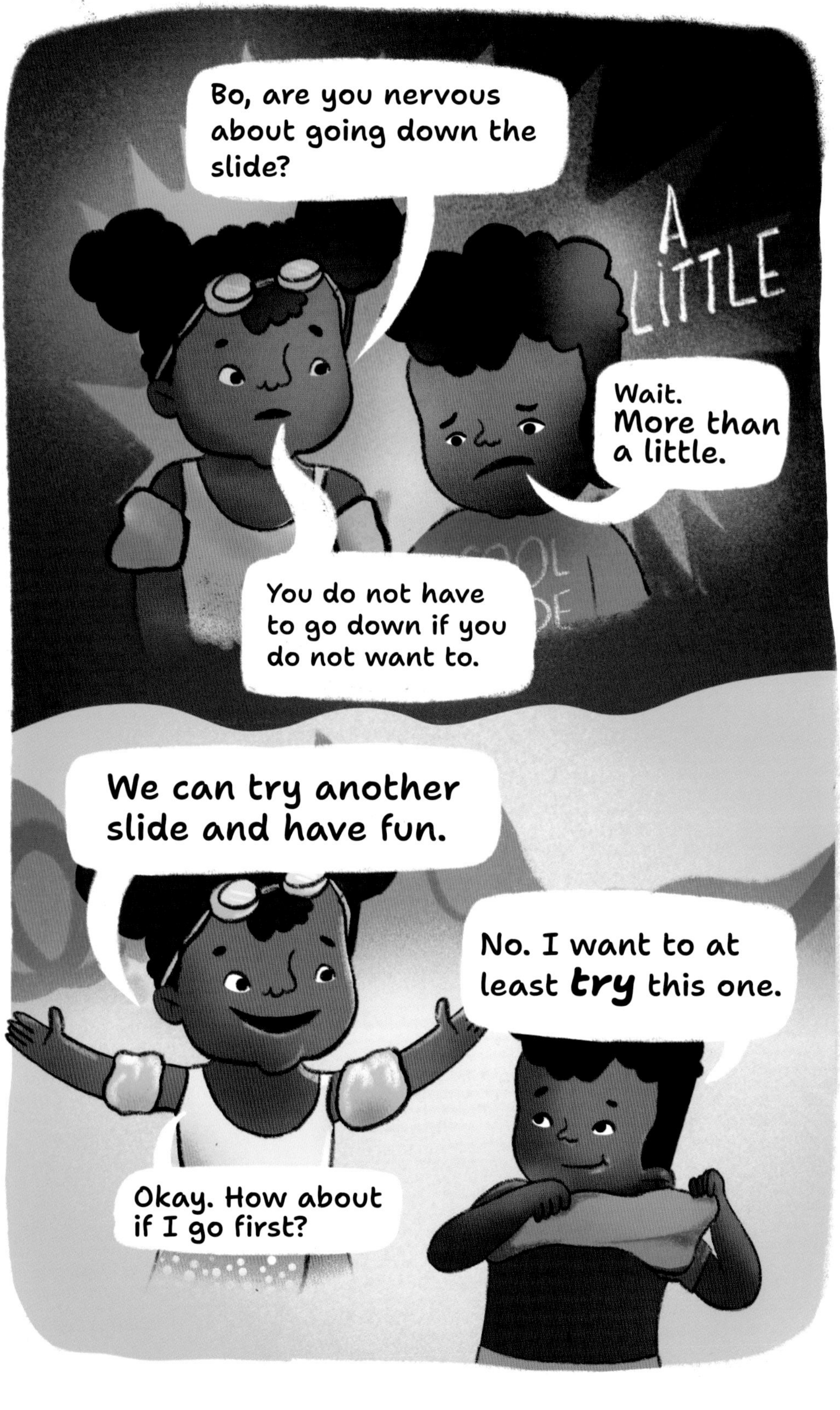
Bo, are you nervous about going down the slide?
A LITTLE
Wait. More than a little.
You do not have to go down if you do not want to.
We can try another slide and have fun.
No. I want to at least **try** this one.
Okay. How about if I go first?

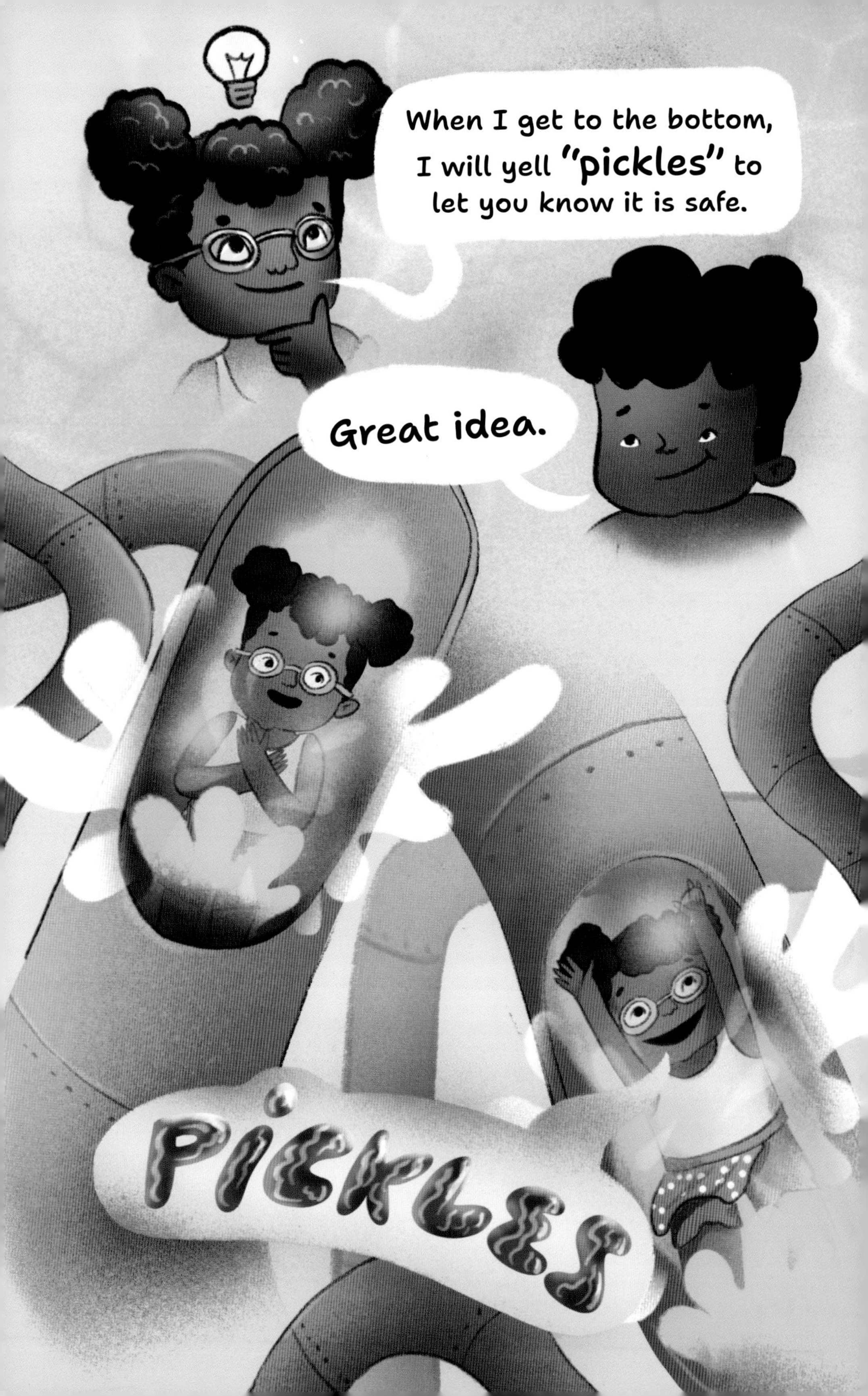
When I get to the bottom,
I will yell "pickles" to
let you know it is safe.
Great idea.
PICKLES

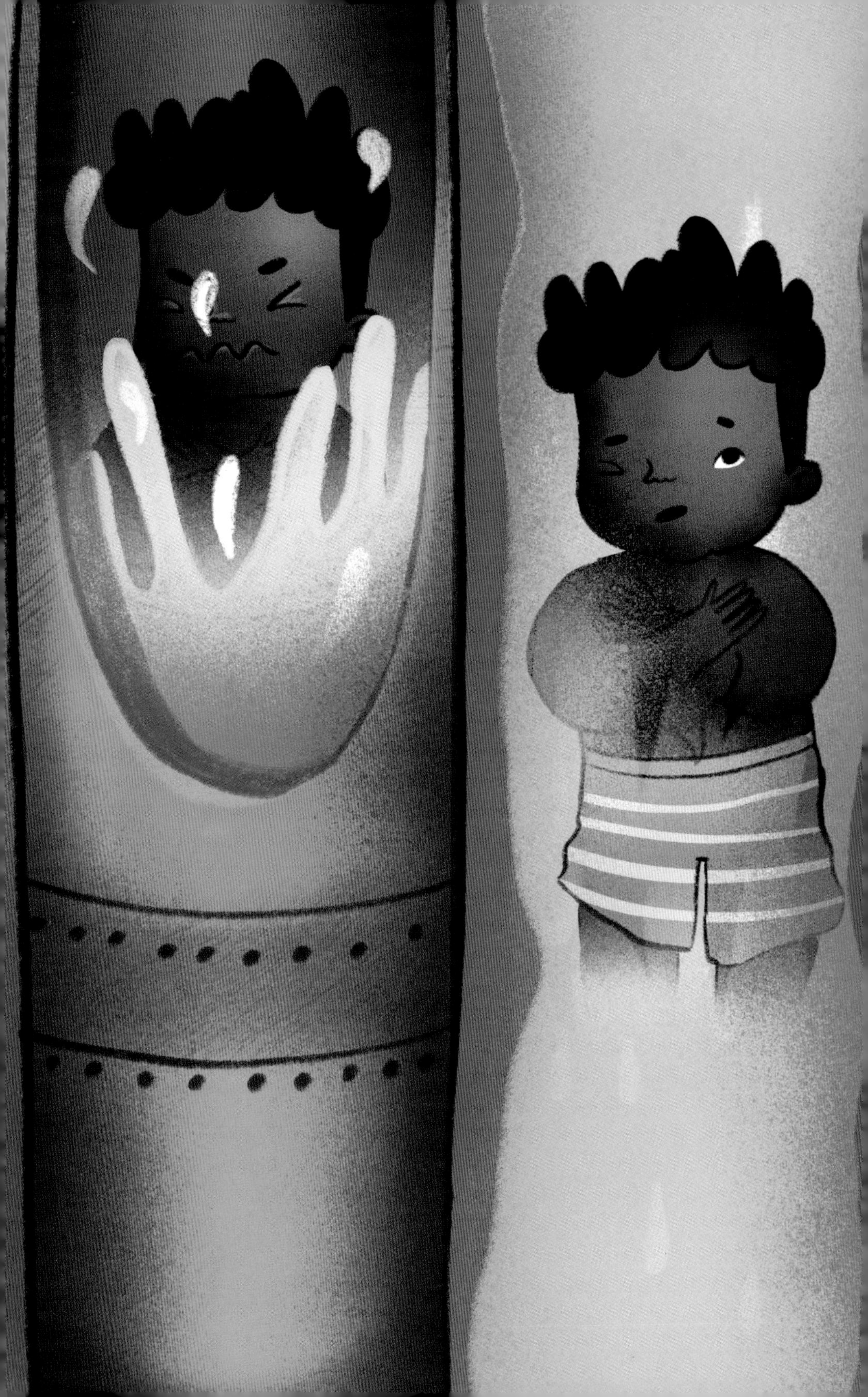

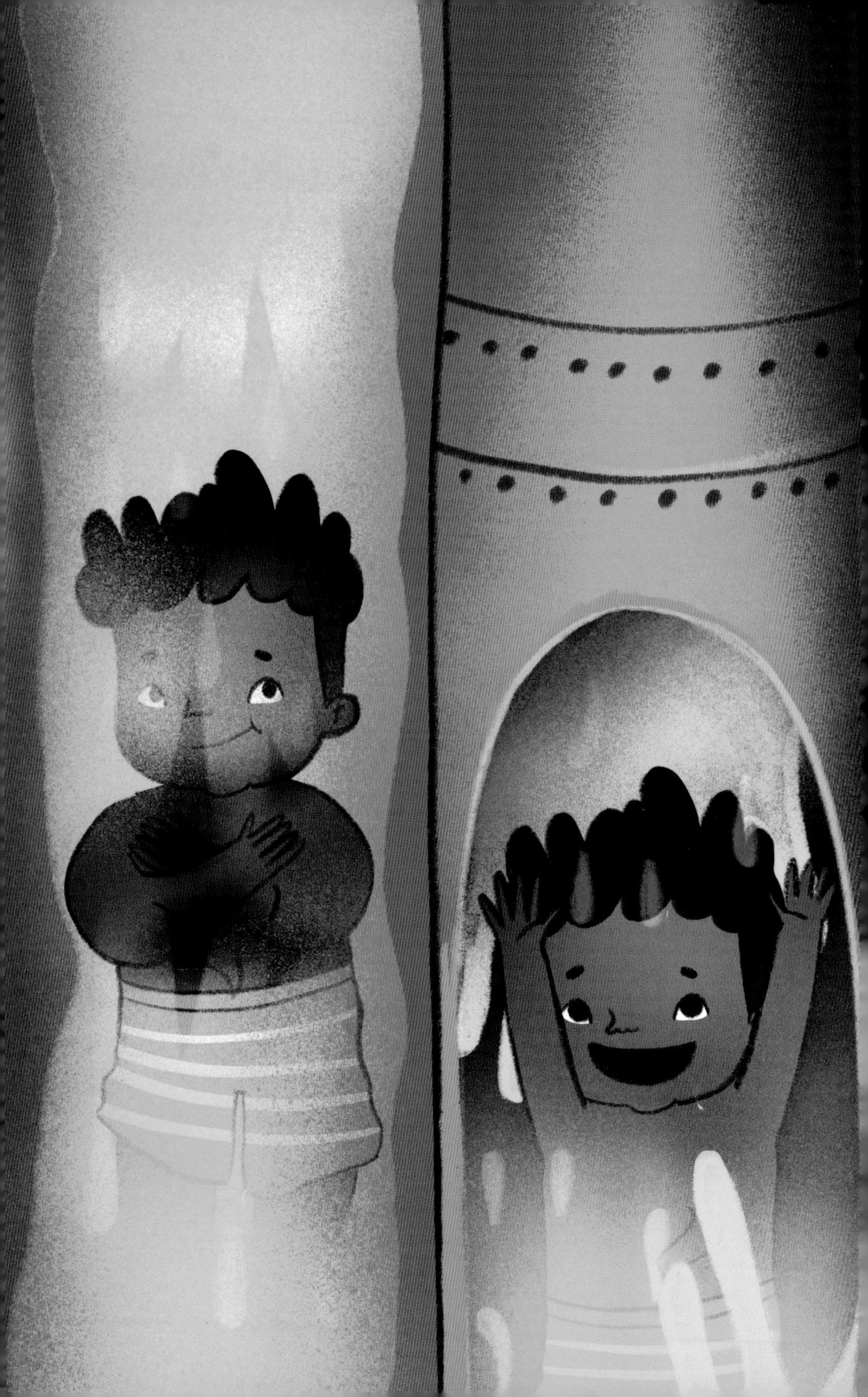

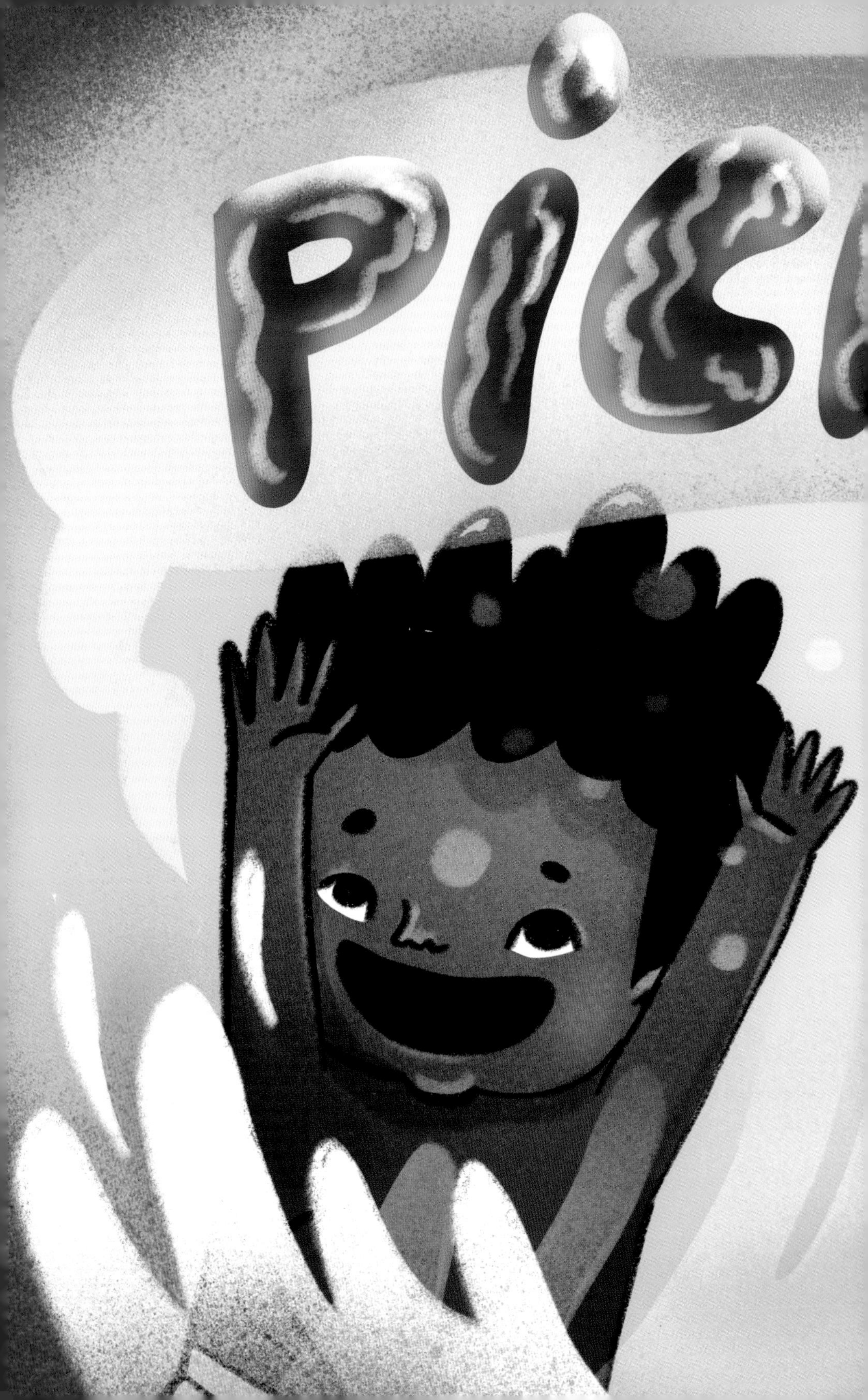

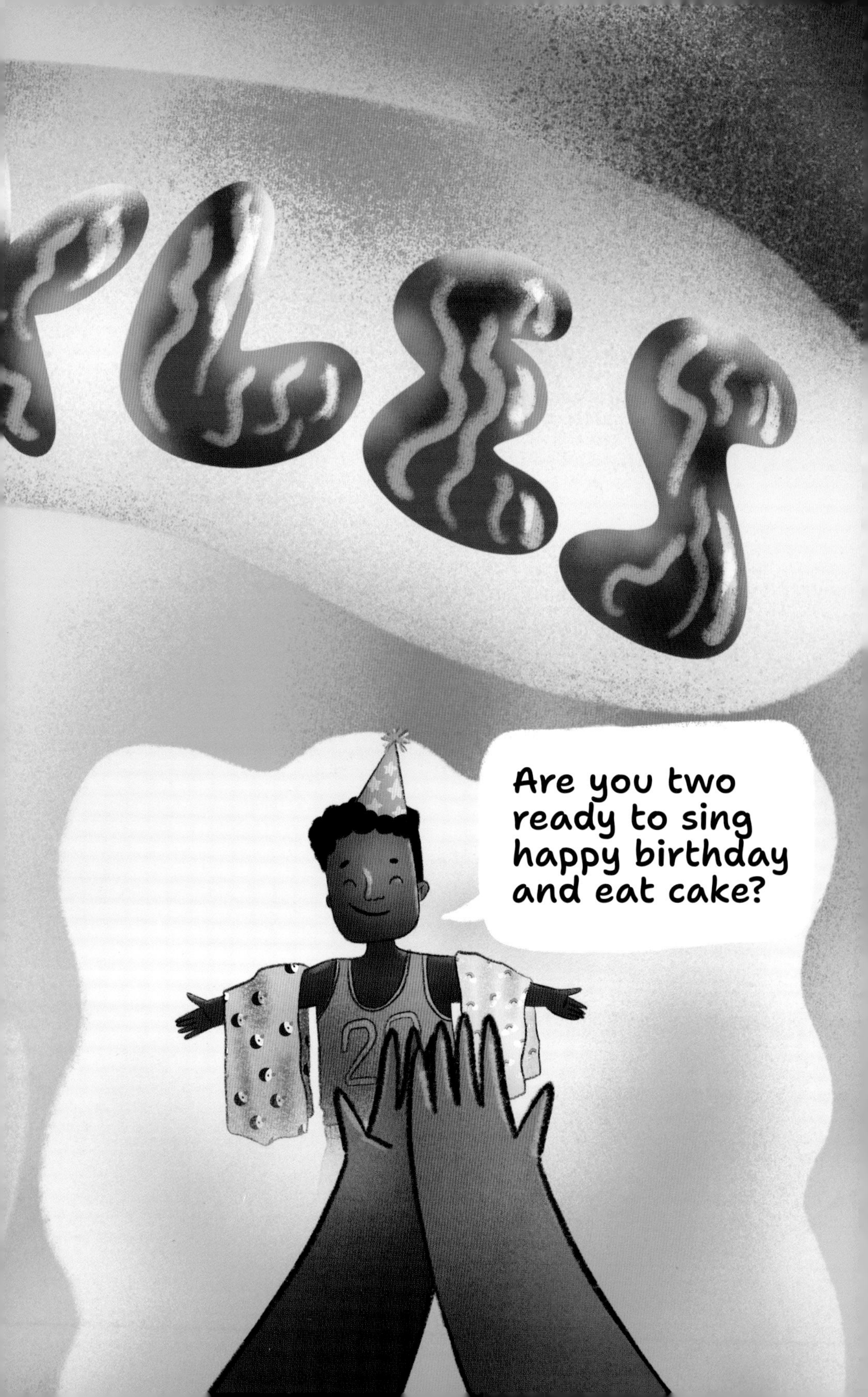
Are you two ready to sing happy birthday and eat cake?

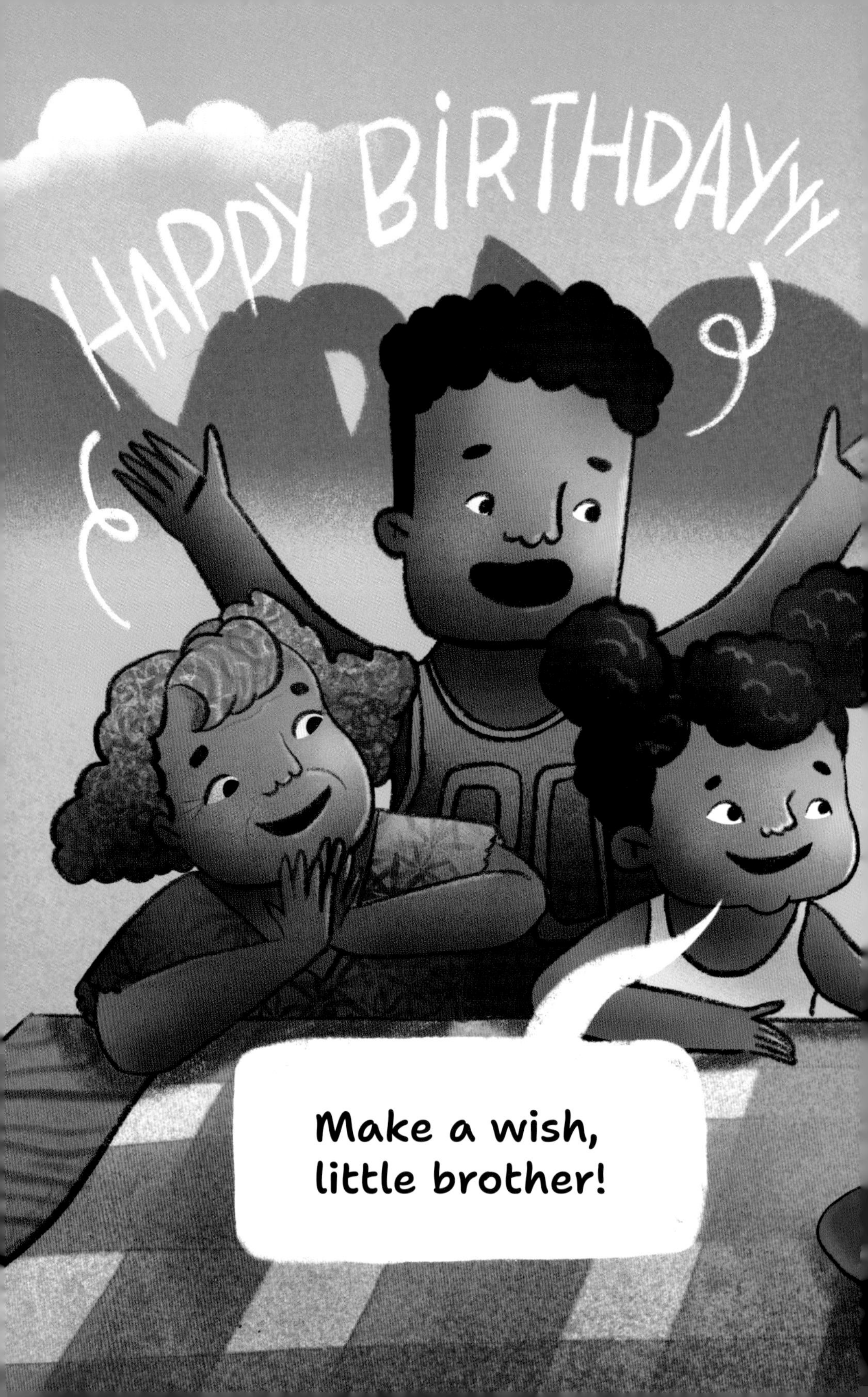
HAPPY BiRTHDAYYY
Make a wish, little brother!

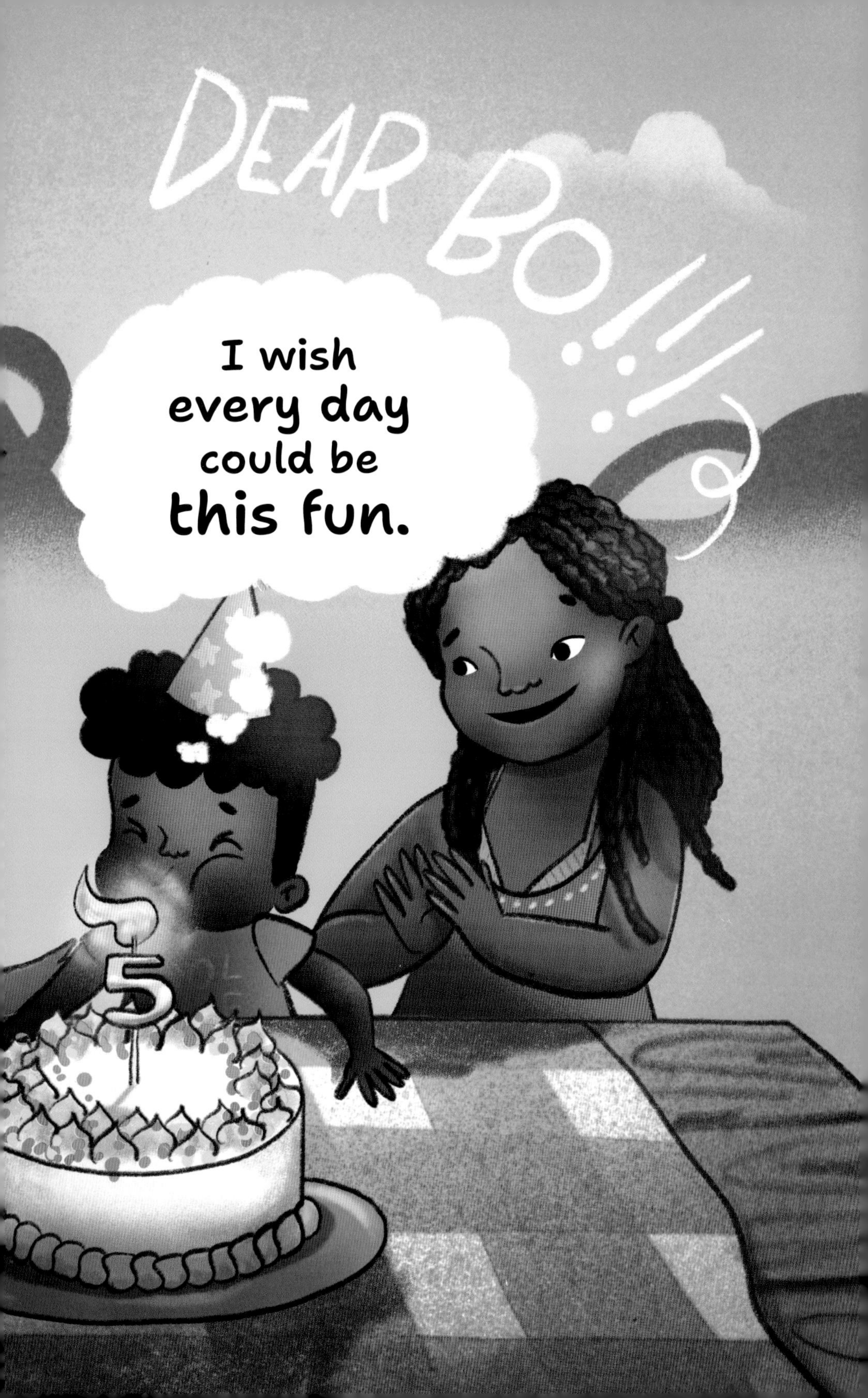
DEAR BO!!!
I wish every day could be this fun.

JESSE BYRD

The most important thing to know about Jesse is that he's an older brother who loves to mess with his younger brother. Bad jokes. Tussling. Aggravating him until he gets a reaction. In this work, Jesse considers himself an artiste.

When he's not doing that (and he does that a lot), he's probably creating stories for young readers.

LAU MORAITI

pronounced "more-eye-tee"

Lau has been a big sister for almost all her life. She loves to play board games whenever her brother visits. As kids, they enjoyed battling at Guess Who? and games of cards.

Lau is an artist from Uruguay, a tiny country in South America. She's a mom who loves to draw stories for kids.

She also loves the color pink, eating pizza, and having many pets.

Use the hashtag **#bigsistercoco** to share YOUR favorite things to do with your siblings!